In the
Shadow of Guilt

Lise Kristine Viken

In the Shadow of Guilt

A mothers struggle to survive, despite the
horror she caused

Fjellgeita forlag AS

Published by:

Fjellgeita forlag AS (Mountaingoat publisher LLC)
Masfjordnes, Norway 2024

www.fjellgeitaforlag.no

Previous books by Lise Kristine Viken:

Pacific Crest Trail – 150 dager på fottur i USA, 2018
(Norwegian edition)

Heretter trenger jeg ingen, 2023
(Norwegian novel)

150 days-the true story of how I lost 88 pound
and became a mountain goat on the
Pacific Crest Trail, 2023

©Lise Kristine Viken

ISBN 978-82-693169-4-0

Editing: Rebecca Allen
Cover design: Fjellgeita forlag AS
Picture: ©Lise Kristine Viken

In the stillness of the mountains,
the whispers of the soul become clear

Introduction

Maja

2007

Some days, nothing makes sense in her head. Her mind buzzes like confused flies in the first spring sun. She can't focus. Slowly, a dreadful darkness grows within her, where everything is black and saturated with hatred.

How long has it been since he left? Packed his things and vanished. Not a single word of goodbye. Just gone. No warning. Empty closets. Even the sofa was gone. She had never cared about it anyway, but now that it's no longer there, it feels incomprehensible. She wants it back, along with him, her greatest love. But now, she is supposed to be without him. He is to become a stranger to her.

If only he would respond to her text messages with something other than "maybe" and "we'll see." She needs something tangible, something she can use, something that can give her the hope she so desperately craves.

The phone pings from the coffee table, but it's not him this time either. The local shopping center wants to inform her about an upcoming sale starting in a few days. As if she cares about that. They can have all the sales they want; she won't be there. She has more than enough to deal with, battling the darkness that has crept back into her.

Psychopath. That's what the doctor had said.

"You have psychopathic traits," he had told her. "The sooner you accept your life with this diagnosis, the better. There is help available: hospitalization, pills, therapy. You can learn to live with it, but you need to take control."

But today, she has no control. She is overtaken by a dark shadow that has infiltrated her system. She is a helpless victim, and there is no one who can save her.

The shadow is creative and inventive. What will it concoct this time? It always starts with "research." The same questions arise. Where is he? What is he doing? Who is he with?

Jealousy grows with the shadow. Together, they bore into the lowest vertebra and work their way up, taking over her brain.

She searches for his name. It's still the same address and the same phone number—the one he has blocked her from.

Now she knows what must be done; the shadow has made its decision. She must confront him.

By the time she gets in the car, it is already dark outside. She knows the way by heart, but she must not get too close, must not be discovered.

She parks the car on a side street a few blocks from the house where he lives. The dark clothes and the hat pulled low over her head provide protection and a shield of anonymity.

Slowly, she approaches the light streaming from the living room windows. Has he drawn the curtains this time, she wonders. It wasn't long since she was here last. Maybe he's forgotten? Maybe he's relaxing, thinking he's finally rid of her? She hears the laughter before she sees her—the woman with the long blonde hair sitting on the sofa. Her sofa. How dare she? Who gave her permission to sit there as if she owned it? Calmly, she moves a little closer, wanting to see better. Needing to know more. Who is she? What is she doing here?

Jealousy is like a dark, sticky lump that settles in her spine.

She feels the hatred towards this disgusting, unbearable, strange creature sitting and laughing on her furniture. Now she leans back, settling in and snuggling up to him like a repulsive, slimy eel. He lets it happen. Opens his arm for this being. Touches her. Laughs with her.

The shadow is too strong. She can't take it anymore. All rational thoughts are gone. Dazed, she staggers away from the horrible sight in the window. Her legs tremble. Her whole body shakes, although it feels paralyzed by shock.

His car is perfectly parked in the lot, backed carefully into the small space allocated for his vehicle. Carefully, she leans against it.

A confrontation is impossible. Not when that creature is here. She doesn't want to show weakness in front of others. Slowly, she crouches down. Tears stream down her cheeks, dripping onto the ground like small raindrops. She collapses onto the gravel, lying as if dead drunk, robbed of any control over herself.

Her fists clench around the pebbles. Almost in a trance, she lifts her hand, full of gravel, up along the fender of the blue Mazda. It makes a sharp scraping sound, but not too loud. She continues across the hood. The gravel feels like a peeling for her. She massages and scrubs, wanting to remove all the pores. She rubs harder and harder, finds some larger stones. It becomes a work of art with long, straight, deep scratches—big squiggles without purpose or meaning. The car endures what should have been her physical pain.

She's done. All she can manage is to half-walk, half-stagger back to her own car. Her mind is blank. Her brain can't focus. Dazed, she gets in and turns the key.

The next morning, she wakes up with a sense that something has happened, something she can't quite grasp. Her hands are red and swollen, but she doesn't understand why.

The sounds of children playing bring her out of her stupor. The sound of her lovely children—the two little heartbreakers. The sun is shining outside, it's the weekend, and her head and heart fill with joy and warmth. All the bad from the night before is gone, erased as easily as hitting "delete" on a keyboard. She doesn't remember it. It's repressed, buried deep in her mind somewhere.

After a long and pleasant breakfast with her two

darlings, the doorbell rings. The oldest opens and calls out, "Mom, you need to come."

Two uniformed policemen are standing outside. They want to know where she was the night before.

She doesn't understand what they mean. She was home with her daughters. They can't possibly think she left them alone. She's convincing, charming, lively. It comes naturally to her.

"Someone vandalized his car," they say. "Gravel and stones have scratched up the paint. It has to be written off—completely destroyed."

The police think she's behind it. She has threatened him before. They don't give up; they're persistent, trying to force her into their version of events.

"Arrest me, then," she says. "Prove it. File a case. Let child services take the kids. That's what you want, isn't it? Maybe he did it himself, trying to make me look bad, make me appear like a bad mother. He's threatened to take the kids before. Haven't you read the case? Coming here and accusing me—I can't understand it. I'm a good mother. I do everything for my children. I've never hurt anyone."

Tears stream down her cheeks. She is devastated by the harsh accusations.

The men drive away and write their reports. They can't believe that the little, sweet woman with the two charmers could have done such a thing. He probably did it himself. They dismiss the case.

Maja

2008

Maja slowly wakes up, unwillingly slipping out of the pleasant dream. She was with him—her greatest love, her first.

They had met in their youth when she started attending local dances after being confirmed. Everyone did it; it was the rule, no exceptions. Parties and fun every Saturday night, and absolution the next day in church.

Fifteen years old and unkissed. Shy. Embarrassed around boys.

Luckily, she had a good friend who had "borrowed" a couple of bottles of Hansa beer from the fridge at home. Hidden behind the large, red community hall, they secretly drank a bottle each. The liquid was brown and didn't smell good. The taste was unpleasant. Two sips of beer, then a sip of cola—that's how they managed to drink it. Young and promising. No clear future plans, just the here and now. Nothing else mattered.

The cigarettes came out; they had pooled their money to buy a ten-pack of Prince Mild. The world was at their feet, and they were ready to conquer it.

She'd never forget the first time she saw him—the blond fringe, the kind eyes, a bit serious, jeans with holes at both knees. He was a few years older than her. Had his driver's license. With a beer in her, she felt invincible, light, and carefree. The shyness and insecurities were gone.

He was sitting on the high wall near the entrance to the hall. When she walked by, he called out to her, having waited for an opportunity. Words weren't necessary; he simply pulled her close and kissed her gently on the lips. Her first kiss. Hesitantly, she returned the kiss as best she could. Exciting and unfamiliar feelings began to emerge. He kissed her again, this time a bit harder.

Maja was lost. She realized that quickly. The rest of the evening, she didn't leave his side once. And when the band played a final slow song, he led her out onto the dance floor and kissed her again and again as they moved slowly to the music.

"Where have you been all my life?" he whispered in her ear.

Dazed by the intoxication of the moment, Maja couldn't respond. All she could do was cling to him and hope that time would stop.

When they finally managed to tear themselves apart, he promised to come back the next time there was a dance in her hometown.

Weeks turned into months. There were more dances at the hall. And each time, she waited for him—in vain. He never showed up. The heartbreak completely overwhelmed her and drained her of all energy. Nothing mattered anymore; she was nothing without him.

Where was he? Why didn't he come to her?

Time passed, and she entered her twenties. Then, one day when she least expected it, he was standing in front of her again. She had reluctantly joined her girlfriends for a night out in town. Her job as a waitress at one of Bergen's hottest restaurants was demanding; she was tired. But she had let herself be persuaded. The shock of seeing him again was quickly replaced by warm feelings, and she didn't ask any questions about why he hadn't shown up all those years ago. Nor did he offer any explanation, but when he kissed her, she forgot everything and let herself be swept away.

Slowly, she pushes the memories aside. Something isn't right; it's too quiet in the house. Then she remembers— the kids are gone. Summer vacation started a few days ago, and they're spending two weeks with him, their father. And Kjersti. Just thinking about her brings pain to her stomach, and nausea rises in her throat. The woman with the blonde hair, the woman who has stolen her life. Maja runs to the bathroom, unable to stop her insides from twisting, and everything comes up as a painful, bitter lump.

The tears come on their own, and she lies in the fetal position on the bathroom floor, between an abandoned stuffed animal and her own clothes, which are piled in a heap on the floor. A strong smell hits her nose. It smells sharply of something that reminds her of the times she went into the woods with the kids and grilled sausages. A bonfire—it smells like a bonfire.

Her mind is in chaos. She can't sort out what she did the day before. The last thing she remembers is enjoying a glass of wine and planning how she would get through the next two weeks alone. Went to bed early. She's pretty sure of that. But the clothes on the bathroom floor suggest that other things might have happened.

Did the shadow visit her yesterday? Desperately, she staggers around the house, searching for more clues. A broken wine glass, red wine stains on the sofa, the front door half-open, charred rubber shoes in the entryway. What has she done this time? Panic threatens, and she decides to check the police's Twitter account. She desperately hopes not to find anything there that could clarify what might have happened, clinging to the thought that she just had a minor episode and burned some yard waste the night before.

The sentence hits her like a punch to the gut. Four people missing after a severe house fire. The fire is under control, but it's not safe for the fire department to search the ruins. It's his house; she recognizes the area, feels it deep in her bones.

Her children. They're gone, lost in a black mass of wood and ruins. The air is knocked out of her, and she collapses to the floor. Her body trembles, and her mind unravels.

Slowly, the realization comes to her—it's her doing. Or it's the shadow that has darkened her mind so many times before. The smell of smoke, the charred rubber shoes—the evidence floods over her like icy snowflakes, settling around her heart.

Her life is over. It's almost as if she's been waiting for this day and welcomes it. She is filled with a strength she didn't know she had, rises from the floor, and slowly walks down the steep stairs to the basement. At the back of the basement storage room, under a pile of planks that serve as camouflage, she finds what she's looking for.

The secret bag. No one else knows about it—not him, not the children, none of her friends. It's her secret.

From now on, she needs no one.

Ingvar

1945

He trembles like an aspen leaf in the wind. The cold rushes through him, burrowing into every tiny pore. It's spring, but it feels like winter. The snow still lies in large drifts across the mighty mountains of Stølsheimen. Yesterday's snowstorm has made the terrain impassable.

For three endlessly long days, he has been lying here, curled up in the damp, gray sleeping bag designed for dry conditions. He knows where he is; these mountains are as familiar to him as the back of his hand. He knows every little nook and cranny.

Today, he feels a bit stronger. The wound from the bullet that hit his shoulder has begun to heal. He knows how lucky he is. The bullet went straight through, leaving only a small, round hole on both sides of his body. The German was not so lucky; Ingvar had hit perfectly, right between the eyes. But the sound of the bullet striking haunts him. That dull thud is forever etched into his young mind.

"It was him or me, and it turned out to be him." Just thinking about everything that has happened in the last few months makes him tremble even more as he lies there.

He was just a boy the day the Germans invaded Norway and took over his hometown of Bergen. It all happened within a few days, difficult days when no one fully understood what was going on. Together with his friend Didrik, he had been down on Harbour-street, observing the marching forces. The sound of soldiers' boots on cobblestones, hundreds of them, echoed far up the sides of the seven mountains that surrounded the city.

At first, it had been a bit exciting. The two boys, with their innocent, childish minds, had no way of sensing the horror that was creeping in. They still ran around the streets with their homemade guns, playing war.

Maybe it wasn't so bad to be invaded by the Germans; maybe life for ordinary working people would get better. Ingvar had overheard his parents talking after he was in bed. But the excitement and optimism soon faded in the little family.

It didn't take many days before the Germans began to make their mark on the city, with new, incomprehensible orders and rules. And, not least, punishment and persecution for those who did not obey, those who thought it was safe enough to protest.

Slowly but surely, resistance grew, and Ingvar felt the hatred building up against the foreign occupying force. Ingvar was an only child. He had grown up in a safe environment with a loving mother and a gentle father. Both parents were born in Masfjorden municipality, with its steep valleys, majestic mountains, and narrow fjords. Times were tough, and like so many others at that time, his parents had migrated to Bergen in search of a better life. They lived in a small apartment on Hillsidestreet, surrounded by other newly established families who also dreamed of a carefree and comfortable life without hunger and misery.

But the ties to Masfjorden were strong, and every summer they took the steamship from Bryggen in Bergen to spend a few weeks in the idyllic surroundings with his grandparents in Masfjordnes. When the war came, they continued to travel to Masfjorden as often as they could. Sometimes Ingvar stayed behind in the countryside to help his grandparents. His parents also felt it was safer for him there.

Despite the difficult times, these were valuable years for the young boy. His grandfather took him hunting and fishing, teaching him everything about surviving on his own in the rugged and hilly Masfjorden mountains and the Stølsheimen mountain area.

The war felt distant when he occasionally spent the night alone under the open sky on a mountaintop. He could lie there and dream himself far away, gazing at the stars and pondering the mysteries of the universe, wondering if there really was a god far up there looking down at him.

The autumn of 1944 was a turning point for Ingvar and his friend. In Didrik's bedroom, no more than a small attic hideaway, they had stashed away a radio. It was strictly forbidden for ordinary people to possess a radio; those discovered faced no mercy and often received a bullet in the forehead on the spot. But the friends listened to broadcasts from London as often as they dared.

The voice on the radio spoke Norwegian; they knew that the Norwegian people, both in the resistance movement and in private homes, were following the broadcasts. With a clear voice, they heard the important message from London that the German occupying forces had decided that all young boys aged sixteen and up would be sent to the Eastern Front to assist the German forces.

Norwegian authorities, together with the Allies, urged all boys in the vulnerable age group to immediately report to the resistance movement and the new units being formed. All boys from Bergen were asked to leave the city immediately and head to Masfjorden, where they would become part of the Norwegian resistance.

The two friends had recently turned seventeen and had long dreamed of being able to help drive the Germans out of the country. Now it was their turn to mobilize, and they didn't hesitate.

Time was short; they knew the Germans were also listening to the broadcasts from London. They had to leave immediately. Ingvar would have liked to go home to say goodbye to his parents, but it was too risky. Instead, he wrote a short letter that Didrik's father promised to deliver.

While Didrik's mother packed food, the boys gathered what little equipment they could find at Didrik's house. Then they set off on foot up the steep stairs of Stoltzekleiven, heading towards an uncertain fate in the Bjørn West Resistance Group.

Maja

2012

Maja stretches as Doffen affectionately rubs against her, purring softly as she lazily scratches him under the chin. The day has yet to break, and the darkness still lingers, but Doffen doesn't mind. All he cares about is curling up next to Maja, enjoying some affection and lots of attention. Cats are nocturnal, stealthily navigating the darkness as they wait for other night creatures to emerge and "play."
Almost every morning, she finds his trophies just outside the door, or sometimes right by the bed—small, dead gray mice. It's as if he's saying, "look how clever I've been."
The day dawns, and sunlight touches her face. Doffen has fallen asleep, exhausted after the intense mouse hunt of the night. It's autumn, and the cold is becoming noticeable, so she has to light the stove every day. Fortunately, she finished stocking up on firewood well in advance this year—they should be fine through the winter. The pantry is also filled to the brim with trout in brine, salted meat, dried mushrooms, blueberry and cloudberry jams, as well as various plants she's dried for spices and herbs.
She has had an interest in harvesting since she was a little girl. In recent years, she has rekindled this hobby

and incorporated it into her daily life. It has actually become a necessity—she needs the vitamins and extra nutrients found in berries and plants to get through the long, cold winter. And with each season, she finds new places and discovers exciting plants that she can use for both medicine and food.

"I'm becoming a real witch. Who would've thought," she said to Doffen one day while standing over the pots, brewing a concoction of caraway, nettle, and dandelion. "There's nothing better than eating what you've caught yourself, right, little mouse hunter?"

But now it's time to get up. Maja gets out of bed, puts on woolen underwear, thick socks, camouflage pants, and the heavy Marius pattern sweater that belonged to her grandmother, Kristine. The gas stove in the corner, where she has organized a small kitchen, is quickly and efficiently lit. She fetched water from the stream the day before. All she needs to do is fill the steel kettle and put it over the heat.

Her morning routines and breakfast have become a ritual that she cherishes—a calm and quiet moment where she doesn't have to think about anything, just be present and wake up slowly and lazily.

After the usual breakfast of oatmeal with berries and nuts, she sits in her grandfather's rocking chair. It has survived both wars and the test of time.

She takes out the small notebook where she writes down everything she has gathered and what more she needs.

Lists and routines are what keep her alive. And

Doffen, of course. Order and structure, along with having someone who needs her.

The sun is shining; it's a beautiful autumn day. She takes the backpack with her harvesting gear and heads out the gray-painted door, locks it, ensures the camouflage—consisting of a casually built stone wall—is still intact, and then squeezes through the narrow passage in the rock face.

The cabin, which is actually a small shelter, is well hidden in a rocky outcrop, slightly elevated—a natural hideaway where no passerby would bother to investigate further. The path up is naturally made of flagstones that have lain in the scree for hundreds of years.

Her thoughts drift back to that dreadful afternoon nearly three years ago. The cat had saved her life back then. Completely unaware of his own heroic deed, of course, and in a way, they might have saved each other.

She had lived in a state of shock, mixed with grief and disbelief, for a year when Doffen entered her life. But on that particular day, something else had also surfaced in her mind—a feeling of an all-consuming darkness calling to her. Or maybe it was the children she heard in her dreams? The nightmares that returned night after night, vivid images she couldn't escape from.

Whatever it was, right then and there, she had made a decision to end her own life. She could no longer live with the knowledge of what she had done. The time had come to sentence herself to death.

The rope was ready. She had chosen the tree, where the branches were thick and strong, sturdy enough to hold a human body. Not that she was particularly heavy.

The past year had seen her lose weight rapidly, leaving her a shadow of her former self. Her hair was cropped unevenly, unwashed, and thinning. Her skin was pale and grayish. Her clothes didn't fit as they should; they hung loosely around her like rags. The decision to end her life felt liberating.

She had moved far from the cabin, following the almost invisible path that led away from the valley, down toward the lowlands and the fjord. It was a route she had followed many times before, but on that day, she had a specific destination in mind.

The goal was a small clearing in the forest, an idyllic spot with a pond surrounded by sporadic birch trees. She had been there before, camping in a tent or lying in a hammock strung between the tall trees, which now were to be used for a very different purpose.

The memories flooded in as she approached. The wind gently tousled her hair, like a light caress from a child's hand, and she thought she heard Solveig's light, trilling laughter. She imagined her wading cautiously on the small sandy patch, with water just above her ankles but still on safe ground. In the background, little Laura appeared. Sweet little Laura with her dark ringlets and chubby legs, toddling around on unsteady feet long before her first birthday. A little charmer who could wrap everyone around her little finger.

Maja arrived at the clearing. The children welcomed her; she could hear them calling and coaxing her, wanting her to join them. The big, sturdy, beautiful birch tree also waited. The leaves still hung green and summery on the branches.

She took the rope out of the old hiking backpack. She didn't dwell much on what she was doing; she acted on an inner voice that told her what to do. It wasn't the shadow; it hadn't been with her since that dreadful night. Icy cold had taken the shadow's place.

She made a slipknot as she had learned it should be done. The other end she threw over one of the sturdy branches. The rope was long, so she secured it to a lower branch.

A stump that had been lying there aging for decades served as a stool.

Maja stepped up onto the stump, took hold of the loop, and slipped it over her head. She wasn't sad; she was neither wistful nor sorrowful. A sense of freedom welled up within her, and she knew that soon everything would be over, and she would be with her beloved children again. Religion had never been a part of her life, but at that moment, she felt the presence of something else, something that gave her a sign that there was something better.

Something wasn't right. Her subconscious picked up on some pitiful, plaintive sounds that didn't come from her. Nor was it the sound of her daughters. Was someone there? Slowly, she slipped out of the trance and became aware of the unfamiliar sound. Now she was sure someone was calling to her. She lifted the loop away from her neck, stepped back, and got a little shock when she saw herself from the outside. What in the world was she doing!

There was the sound again. Maja stepped down from the stump and focused on locating where it was coming from. She moved away from the pond, slowly approaching a large, gray rock. And there, just behind the rock, she saw it—a small, scruffy, gray and white creature, still a baby, clearly abandoned by its mother. She sat down and stretched out her hand. The tiny kitten sniffed at her cautiously, then stuck out a small tongue as if to taste and assess any potential danger, but it was so starved for contact that it showed no signs of fear. Not long after, it snuggled into her lap, curled up, and started to purr.

Maja settled with the little kitten in her lap. Tears streamed down her cheeks as she wept quietly.

Just minutes ago, her life would have been over. But she was called back at the last moment. Perhaps it was meant to be.

Was she supposed to find this creature? She couldn't take her own life now. That would be sentencing the cat to death as well. Hadn't she caused enough suffering already? Was she to have more lives on her conscience?

"We need to find you some food, little friend. There's plenty of canned milk at the cabin; you'll come with me there," she said to the little one.

Not long after, she had packed up the rope and put the backpack on her shoulders. She placed the kitten in a cloth that she tied around her waist. It curled up and remained quiet until they reached the hidden cabin. Maja found a can of condensed milk from the stash and poured it into a bowl. The little one eagerly lapped it all up, utterly famished. Then he climbed back into her lap, settled in comfortably, and they both fell asleep.

Maja

2013

For five years, Maja has lived alone in the mountain wilderness. Five years without anyone discovering her existence. Five years without human contact.

In the secret cabin, the provisions have started to dwindle. She will probably make it through the next winter, but from experience, she knows that the best thing one can do in life is to be prepared for anything, preferably for the worst. That's what her grandfather taught her. Good old Grandpa.

Her grandfather was a man of few words, but for Maja, that didn't matter. They understood each other without the need for deep conversations. Instead, he showed her how to appreciate the peace and silence of the wild and beautiful mountains, far from the noise and bustle of the city. Everything she knew about survival, nature, and the mountains, she had learned from Ingvar. He was also the one who let her in on the big secret—after his death, when she inherited information containing the coordinates and description of how to find the cabin. The fact that the cabin was off the beaten track meant that, to this day, no one has discovered it.

But even though it is well hidden and located high in the mountains, the cabin is within reach of several small villages, marked hiking trails and cabins.

Today, Maja's destination is one of the many Norwegian Trekking Association (or DNT) cabins in Stølsheimen. Not the most popular cabin—it's a good day's hike from the nearest road, and she feels quite confident that no other visitors will show up on an ordinary weekday.

She approaches the cabin slowly and takes a break well out of sight of any potential onlookers. She uses the time to observe if there is any activity, if there's smoke coming from the chimney. Then she takes a chance and heads towards the entrance. No shoes on the steps—a good sign. The hook on the outside of the door is in place. That settles it; no one is here, she's safe.

Inside the cabin, she takes a quick look around before starting the task she came for. Most DNT cabins are equipped with a supply of provisions. Here you can find many goodies, everything from canned reindeer meatballs to chocolate spread. The system is based on honesty and trust; what you use, you must record and pay for yourself. Maja is careful to settle her accounts.

She fills her backpack with treats like canned peaches, vanilla sauce, and chocolate cookies, but also crispbread, liver pâté, and canned ham. The backpack becomes quite heavy, but she doesn't mind.

Just as she's about to put the last packet of pea soup in her backpack, the outer door moves.

In walks a tall man in his thirties. He has dark hair, a tan, and looks like the very symbol of a fit, mountain-savvy Norwegian. He squints a little to adjust his eyes to the dim light in the cabin before spotting Maja, who is half-hidden behind the door to the provision storage.

"Hello, is someone here?" he exclaims with a big smile, before setting his backpack down and beginning to untie his black military hiking boots.

Maja has frozen in place. Panic washes over her, and she spends a little extra time tying her backpack straps. After what feels like an eternity, she manages to regain control of herself, and with her head down and avoiding eye contact, she sneaks past him. A small "hello" is all she manages.

"Have you walked far?" he asks, following her into the small living room. He doesn't wait for an answer but continues to chat about how far he has walked, how incredibly beautiful the mountains are, and how he's looking forward to relaxing in the cabin with a good meal.

Small talk has never been Maja's strong suit. Fortunately, he doesn't seem to care much that he's not getting any answers. It's as if he understands that she's not the talkative type. Maja has to register her visit in the cabin logbook. Instead of giving her own name, she writes Kristine, after her grandmother, and Fjellstad, as that's the only name she can think of at the moment. She leaves the address field blank, then places plenty of money and a list of the items she has taken in an envelope, and pushes it down into the safe slot.

"I have to get going," she excuses herself, nearly storming out of the cabin. Outside on the steps, she has to take a few minutes to put on her shoes.

"Are you heading towards Voss, perhaps?" asks the man, who has followed her out and introduces himself as Knut.

"Something like that," Maja says quietly before finally getting her shoes on and hurrying off in the direction of the next DNT cabin towards Voss.

It's not the right way, but she has no choice. It will be a small detour back to the cabin, but Maja knows the area like the back of her hand and is blessed with a good sense of direction.

Back on the steps, Knut is standing. He wonders a bit about her reserved behavior. Most people who meet in the mountains tend to be more talkative than average and social. There was something familiar about her, but he couldn't quite put his finger on it. Back in the living room, he finds her name in the logbook.

Kristine Fjellstad.

He makes a note on his phone to check the name when he gets home.

Maja

2014

Spring is on the way. The snow is melting, and the days are becoming brighter and milder. Doffen is overjoyed to be outside, reveling in the thaw after an exceptionally cold winter, when temperatures often plunged well below freezing in January. The winter has also been particularly hard on Maja. Since the unexpected encounter at the DNT cabin last fall, she hasn't been quite herself. The constant worry that someone might discover her or the hidden cabin has weighed heavily on her. Yet, her meeting with Knut has also stirred something deep within her.

Maja hasn't had a boyfriend since Morten, the father of her children, left her. The past few years have been consumed by grief and survival, leaving no room for anything else. But seeing that handsome man awakened feelings she had long suppressed—the need for warmth and care from another person, someone to lie close to, the physical contact between two people who care about each other.

To distract herself from the impossible, Maja has filled her days with tasks. She refuses to think about the future, wanting only to exist in the present, in this self-imposed exile, a life free from obligations and responsibilities, free from other people. It's her eternal punishment. Yet, she can't completely ignore the longing for companionship, care, and close contact.

Earlier this winter, she had gone back to the same DNT cabin. The snow was deep, making encounters with other people unlikely during that time. She knew from experience that the cabin would be closed for the winter, and it was rare for anyone to venture into the mountains during the harshest months in Stølsheimen. So, she took the chance, bringing skis and a sled, ensuring the weather wasn't perfect so that fresh snow would cover her tracks.

Armed with a shovel and the universal DNT key, which she had acquired years ago, she set off. The snow was firm and fine, making the journey easier. When she reached the cabin, she found it buried in snowdrifts, but after an hour of shoveling, she was able to open the door. The cabin was freezing, but she hadn't planned to stay long.

The provisions weren't as plentiful as last time, but it felt like a luxury to Maja. She packed her backpack and sled with canned goods, soup packets, spreads, and crispbread.

Knowing such a large shopping spree might raise suspicions, Maja took her time filling out several forms with different names and varying amounts of money. She didn't want to be a thief, but she needed to cover her tracks and ensure no one suspected someone was hiding in the mountains. Before leaving, she had a sudden impulse. The guestbook lay open, and she flipped back to the page from her last visit. She found his name and read the few words he had written. A jolt of surprise went through her.

"Thanks for the stay, always nice to be here. I'll be back in the spring. Maybe we'll meet again, Kristine?" It was signed Knut Langholm.

This morning, her thoughts revolve around Knut. He seems to want to see her again. Maja has lived alone for so long, drowning out all thoughts and feelings. Could she ever return to a normal life? It would mean confronting what she has done, turning herself in to the police, and accepting her punishment.

The thought is tempting; she feels she deserves all the punishment she can get. But the process would be so traumatic that she can't bear to think about it. The memories and images of her children would haunt her relentlessly. The media would feast on the case, judging her and portraying her as the monster she believes herself to be.

Maja sits down next to Doffen, who has curled up comfortably on the old wooden bench. She gently strokes his head and scratches him under the chin. The cat begins to purr contentedly, and Maja tries to focus on the present, on daily tasks, on survival. Her life is here; this is her punishment: a self-imposed existence under harsh conditions. Prison would be too easy, too lenient. Her crime is unforgivable. The best thing for everyone is that she remains hidden and lives an eternally secluded life.

Ingvar

1945

A week has passed, and Ingvar is spending most of his time huddled in his sleeping bag, trying to stay warm. The meager supply of provisions—dried bread and salted fish—is nearly gone. Tomorrow, he knows he must make his way back to civilization, despite the risks. He doesn't know if the Germans are still searching for him. His thoughts drift back to his first meeting with Bjørn West.

They had received a counter-order to report to Matre, only to be sent up into the mountains. The equipment they had was ill-suited for the harsh conditions they encountered as they crossed the tree line and climbed the steep stone steps at Stegane, steps that had been built over a century ago. Now, the resistance was using them to reach the heights as quickly as possible.

Their initial quarters were in an old mountain hut—uninsulated, cramped, with several men squeezed into tiny rooms. Food was scarce, and the dry biscuits they possessed were rationed to the point of near starvation.

Tobacco and camaraderie became their only salvation. All who had escaped the Germans' plan to send them to the Eastern Front felt a deep bond. They spent their days dreaming of the final battles, mobilizing Norway, resisting the German occupation, and reclaiming their homeland.

But they were in need of food, ammunition, and better equipment. They had strict orders not to contact the local population to avoid German reprisals. But after months of near starvation, they had no choice.

In Stordalen, they were welcomed with open arms. Food and lodging were provided without question, and Bjørn West found its new headquarters there.

For a time, the comrades enjoyed life high in the mountains. Food was plentiful, and they helped with hunting. More and more airdrops began to arrive from England, bringing food and ammunition. But one of these drops fell into German hands, causing the enemy to suspect something was happening in the mountains. Patrols from the village of Matre became more frequent. During a reconnaissance mission, Didrik and Ingvar unexpectedly witnessed one of their comrades being shot.

Eventually, fierce battles ensued between the Germans and the Norwegians. Many Germans fell, though the Norwegians also sustained losses. In Bergen, negotiations were underway; the war on the continent was winding down. The Germans were withdrawing from several places, and there were rumors that it might all be over soon.

Then, the order came for Bjørn West to cease hostilities and retreat from the mountain. Ingvar and his comrade were among the last to leave Stordalen on skis. They hadn't gone far before they were ambushed by a German patrol seeking revenge for their fallen comrades in Stølsheimen.

To Ingvar's horror, Didrik was shot by multiple bullets. Ingvar managed to take cover behind a large rock, but he wasn't safe. A German soldier was approaching, just meters away.

During his time with the Home Guard, Ingvar had learned that surprise was one of the most effective strategies.

In a split second, he recalled the commander's words:

"If you can surprise, you have the advantage on your side."

Adrenaline surged through him as he sprang from behind the rock, aimed, and fired. The look of shock on the German's face was unmistakable. In those few seconds, Ingvar had the upper hand. But before he could move again, a sharp pain shot through his left shoulder—another bullet from a German soldier had struck him.

Still running on adrenaline, Ingvar crawled away, focusing on survival. He managed to gain a good lead on the Germans, disappearing into the rugged, snow-covered mountains.

Now, alone in a hidden rock crevice, Ingvar has plenty of time to think about his parents back in Bergen. He imagines them sitting in their kitchen, drinking substitute coffee—real coffee is a luxury they can't afford. Are they thinking of him?

He recalls the letter he wrote in haste.

Dear Mom and Dad,

Now it's my turn to mobilize, and I'm doing so without hesitation. Finally, something is happening. It makes me sad that I won't have time to say goodbye, but we have no time to lose; the enemy is on our heels. You are always in my thoughts. If I should meet a bad end and lose my life, I do so for you and for our homeland. Please don't worry, know that I love you both very much.

With love, Ingvar

He sincerely hopes his parents received the letter and that his mother isn't worrying too much. The guilt of Didrik's death tears at him. If only he had been more careful and more vigilant, perhaps they both could have escaped. What must Didrik's parents think of him?

The uncertainty about his best friend's fate—though deep down he knows the truth—tears Ingvar apart. The clawing guilt in his chest is more painful than the wound in his shoulder.

Suddenly, in the cold winter night, Ingvar hears a voice. At first, he thinks it's just his imagination, a trick of his mind. But then he hears it again.

"Ingvar, are you here?" someone whispers.

A figure emerges—the sight is one he will never forget. His dear grandfather has found him. He is finally safe.

"The war is over; you're coming home, my boy," his grandfather says, tears in his eyes.

Maja

2014

Summer is waning, and autumn is announcing its arrival with a few last mild days. Nature has already begun to adapt to the coming season, with the terrain showing slight hints of color change in red, ocher, orange, and yellow. Soon, the first snowflakes will fall, covering the highest mountain peaks with their white blankets.

Earlier this summer, during one of her daily harvesting trips, Maja noticed some sheep grazing high up on a slope. A large eagle circled just above, eyeing one of the lambs. Suddenly, it swooped down, sinking its talons into the young sheep. Panic broke out among the animals, bleating and scattering in all directions. The lamb quickly proved to be too large for the eagle, which struggled to carry it away.

Maja was horrified by the spectacle. Feeling pity for the little animal, she decided to act. Armed with several sharp stones, she approached the scene. Her first throw sailed just over the eagle's head, causing it to release its grip. But it was too late for the lamb. The talons and powerful beak had inflicted too much damage, and it died in her arms.

Maja, who had never been particularly fond of hunting or slaughtering, mourned the lamb. But the practical side of her, honed after years of fending for herself in the wilderness, knew there was no point in dwelling on it. The lamb was dead, and she needed food. Fortunately, she had learned how to butcher animals from her grandfather, who had taken her on small game and deer hunts since she was young.

Even back then, she had mourned the animals they killed, but her grandfather always assured her it was the way of nature.

She took the knife out of her backpack and set to work. When she was finished, she packed the butchered parts into bags, took the ear tag that identified the sheep's owner, and threw it off a cliff. She wished she could explain the incident to the farmer, but when the autumn sheep gathering was over, they would discover the lamb was missing and assume it had fallen off a cliff or been taken by a predator.

Back at the shelter, she hung the meat to dry under the roof at the entrance.

For Maja, autumn is a busy time. The berry season is in full swing, and she spends most of her days harvesting and picking. After several years in the mountains, she has found the best spots, secret patches where lingonberries, cloudberries, and blueberries abound, as if waiting just for her to harvest them.

In recent weeks, she has ventured far from the shelter. Equipped with a backpack, provisions, and plastic bags for the berries, she has spent many nights sleeping under the open sky. Several of her secret gathering places are in the lowlands, and although the evenings are still bright, and she could make it home before dark, she finds it especially liberating to lie down in a warm sleeping bag right on the heather.

Every evening, she gazes at the stars, unaware that her grandfather used to do the same. In her thoughts, she imagines that her children are somewhere up there, happy, waiting for her. The pain of losing her beloved children has not subsided, but as the years have passed, she has learned to cope. Still, there are days when she curls up in a fetal position and sobs for hours. The anniversaries are the worst—their birthdays, the holidays, the day they died.

She pushes away the heavy thoughts and focuses on picking the last of the blueberries before night falls. From the small hill where she is located, she suddenly hears voices. Maja crouches down and sneaks closer to the edge. There, no more than a hundred meters away, by a small pond, she sees a young couple setting up camp for the night.

It's not the first time she has observed people in nature, but she is always fascinated. Instead of pulling away, retreating to safety, and putting some distance between herself and the strangers, she stays and watches the girl and boy, who look to be in their twenties. She turns away with a smile when the couple strips off all their clothes and jumps into the pond.

"Not much modesty in those two," she thinks.

But then again, they are completely unaware that

someone is lying in the bushes watching them.

Before darkness falls, the boy starts a fire, and Maja sees them grilling sausages for dinner. It's not long before an empty wine bottle lies in the heather. The mood changes suddenly as their voices rise, and the young couple begins to argue.

From her hiding place, Maja sees the girl shove the boy, who responds by slapping her across the cheek with the flat of his hand. The girl collapses, turns away, and starts to cry. It doesn't take long before the boy gathers himself and kneels in front of the girl, begging for forgiveness. The whole incident hasn't taken long, and from the sounds coming from the tent a little later, Maja realizes they have made up.

Afterward, Maja can't shake the incident from her mind. Something has surfaced in her thoughts, an unwelcome idea, a memory repressed far back in her consciousness. A picture of a hand pushing her against a wall. A voice whispering that she is worthless, that she is unfit to be a mother, and that the children don't need her.

That night, she sleeps restlessly, tossing and turning until the first rays of sunlight signal a new day. As she lies in the heather, her thoughts drift back to her time with Morten. The early days, before the children came.

She was only twenty when he appeared in her life for the second time, sweeping her off her feet. Never before had she been so happy. After just a few weeks, they got married, and she moved into his house.

It didn't take long before Maja became pregnant. Morten received the news with such joy that she felt she loved him even more. The next day, he came home from work with a large bouquet of red roses and the book *Everything About the Child*.

"Now we're going to be a proper family," he declared happily.

For Maja, the pregnancy was an exhausting ordeal. Morning sickness dragged on for months, making every day a struggle. She did everything she could to keep Morten from worrying and tried her best to hide how she was really feeling. She got up early, made coffee and breakfast, and packed his lunch for work.

She herself couldn't bear to eat or drink, but curled up in bed as soon as he had driven off.

When they had married, they'd agreed Maja wouldn't work but would stay at home.

"A man's duty is to provide for his wife and children. That's how it was in my upbringing, and that's how I want us to have it," he'd told her with a slightly authoritative tone early one Sunday morning after she had served him coffee in bed.

High on the rush of love, Maja hadn't thought much about the new role she was taking on. Ever since her grandfather had died a few years earlier, she had been lonely. She longed for someone to care for, someone she could spoil, but also someone who cared about her and appreciated what she did. So Maja had no reservations about being a home-maker at a time when the traditional housewife role was long gone.

When did the idyll begin to crumble? Small cracks of doubt, uncertainty, a glimpse here and there that not everything was as it should be. Was it the unspoken words, the incomplete sentences, the small, imperceptible accusations that sneaked in between all the good?

Maja shakes off the gloomy thoughts and opens her sleeping bag. The sun is shining from a clear sky, and it's starting to get warm. She has gathered as many berries as she can carry.

It's a short day's walk back to the shelter, so she packs up the little camping gear she has and takes one last look down at the two youths. The tent flap is still closed, and there are no voices to be heard. Maja quietly withdraws.

A few hundred meters from the shelter, she is greeted by a happy Doffen.

"Did you miss me?" she asks the cat, who rubs against her legs.

Doffen responds with a loud purr as she bends down to scratch his head.

"Of course you missed me. I missed you too. What would we do without each other?" She smiles as she walks toward the base of the stone steps leading up to the hideout.

Inside the shelter, everything is just as it was when she left, except for some bone and skin remnants from several mice, a sure sign that Doffen is guarding the place and can take care of himself. A small tunnel in the wall, right by the front door, serves as Doffen's private entrance, allowing him to come and go as he pleases. In winter, when the cold bites hardest and the snow lies in deep drifts, she closes the small hatch to keep the cold out and the cat in.

Maja fills the largest pot with water, lights the gas stove, and sets the water to boil. She has already prepared the old nostalgic Norwegian glass jars, which stand in a row, ready to be filled with delicious home-made blueberry and cloudberry jam.

Her grandfather taught her how to make preserves. Every summer and autumn, for as long as she could remember, they would harvest and preserve both berries and fruits. Much of it came from their own garden, but also from what they found in the mountains.

She takes out the bag of blueberries, grabs an empty plastic bowl, and sits down on a stone slab outside.

Carefully, she digs her hand into the bag, lifts a handful of berries, and gently picks away small bits of twigs and heather.

"You mustn't eat the berries, or there won't be enough for the jam," her grandfather's friendly but slightly stern voice echoes in her mind.

Even though she knows it isn't allowed, she can never resist tasting. It's become a regular routine. A smile creeps onto her face as she pictures her grandfather trying to be strict with her. She was never intimidated, though, and would keep sneaking a berry or two when he wasn't looking.

Inside the cabin, the water is boiling. She carefully

places the jars and lids into the pot for sterilization. Once the process is done, she pours the boiling water into a metal bucket. It can be used for both washing up and a refreshing bucket shower when the jam is finished.

She has never been vain, but she does appreciate being clean. She plans to make her own soap. She has an idea of which plants to use but needs to experiment a bit before she can come up with a product she's satisfied with. In the meantime, she has several bottles of old Timotei shampoo stored in the cabin.

Freshly showered and clean, she sits down to check her body for ticks. The little annoying bloodsuckers are a constant companion after several days of crawling around in bushes and undergrowth. And sure enough, a couple of them have latched onto the inside of her thigh.

Maja carefully removes them with tweezers. Her body has never shown any reaction to ticks or other insects, but the concern is always there. What would happen if she became seriously ill? It's not just a matter of grabbing her mobile phone and calling for help. Would she be able to reach people in time?

So far, she has only experienced minor injuries and colds—nothing that paracetamol or first aid couldn't fix. But what if she falls off a cliff and breaks something? Then she would be lying there helpless, with no search party coming to find her because no one misses her. The thought is depressing.

"There's no point in thinking negatively. Whatever

happens, happens. We'll take it as it comes, right, Doffen?" she says aloud.

She doesn't get a response.

Maja

2015

It is December. Outside the cabin, the wind howls like a pack of wolves hunting their prey. The first snowstorm of the year is raging, and white flakes swirl endlessly, searching for a place to settle. Everything is white, as far as the eye can see.

Stølsheimen is not a place to be trifled with, as anyone who has inadvertently gotten lost here on a winter night knows. Suddenly, you can find yourself in life-threatening danger, and just one misstep can separate a person from the living or the dead. Stories circulate about people who have disappeared, never to be found again. Countless places in the mountain wilderness can lead straight to death—falling off a cliff into an unknown abyss, or slipping on ice and vanishing into one of the many deep mountain lakes, forever condemned to a cold, watery grave.

Inside the cabin, Maja and Doffen are cozy and warm. The heat from the wood stove spreads throughout the small room, which serves as both kitchen, living room, and sleeping area. Maja has tucked her legs under herself and lounges in her grandfather's old, homemade rocking chair. A large sheepskin adds comfort and makes it extra cozy. The cat has curled up into a little ball on the quilt draped over her bed.

For three whole days, they have been snowed in. The storm makes it impossible to move even a meter outside. The snow lies in large drifts, covering almost the entire entrance. To pass the time, Maja has decided to start a diary, documenting both minor and major events from the days spent with Doffen. She notes down the weather, like an almanac, keeping track of the days of the week. Not that it matters much whether it's Monday or Saturday, but routines on different weekdays make a big difference in her lonely life. She wonder if she should write an autobiography, a manifesto to leave behind in the cabin. Someday, perhaps someone will discover the hidden door in the rock. Maybe they will find her remains.

"Imagine how exciting it would be for them if they also found a diary," she says aloud, glancing at Doffen.

There is so much she doesn't remember from the time with Morten—days when everything was dark, and the darkness became a refuge. Vague episodes she can't quite anchor in reality. But if she writes down her thoughts, maybe she can untangle her life, find some clues that could help her understand.

She is still terrified of the shadow. What if she conjures it back? She decides to take the risk and lets her thoughts drift back to happier times.

Solveig was born at the Kvinneklinikken, the women's clinic in Bergen, on a freezing January morning. Maja had curled up in pain all night long. She had never imagined that giving birth could hurt so much. It took a long time before the midwife finally declared that she needed to push; a small child was eager to enter the world. Not long after, the newborn's first cries filled the room.

No book in the world could have prepared Maja for the feelings that overwhelmed her when she held the little bundle in her arms for the first time. She couldn't get enough of looking at the round face, the tiny wrinkles, the grimaces, the minuscule toes and fingers. Exhausted from the birth, tears streamed down her cheeks. The lump in her throat grew larger the more she gazed at her newborn daughter.

"This is what love at first sight is," she had said to the little child. "Nothing can compare to this feeling. No one in the world shall ever hurt you; I will protect you from all dangers. You are a part of my soul, my precious treasure."

From the very first moment, Maja was absorbed in her role as a mother. Her days were filled with breast-feeding, changing diapers, washing clothes, cooking, and cleaning. Even at night, she had to be on hand as the little one demanded her attention. She fully embraced her role as the perfect housewife.

Morten demanded a certain standard; he had shown her that on several occasions. One day, early in their relationship, Maja had folded towels and placed them in the bathroom cabinet. Later that day, after Morten had showered, he called her.

"You need to fold them properly, and the seam shouldn't show; the towels must be stacked correctly."

Maja laughed a little, thinking he was very particular. A cold stare was all she received in return.

A few weeks before she got pregnant, they had spent a romantic evening at home, and Morten tearfully told her about his own upbringing.

"My father used to beat me. It took nothing to trigger him; I think just my existence was enough," he said with a trembling voice. "Once, I was late for dinner because my bike had a flat tire, and I had to walk home. By the time I got home, my mother had cleared the table. My father was waiting for me in the living room. This time, he had taken off his belt. He ordered me to pull down my pants, and I had to lean over the dining table. The blows rained down on my backside. I don't know what was worse, the humiliation of being beaten or the pain. It took weeks before I could sit properly again."

Maja didn't know what she could do for Morten; his tough stories about a childhood marked by violence and threats touched her heart. Her own upbringing had been good, with a grandfather who loved her dearly. Never once had he laid a hand on her.

Now she wanted to be the one who took care of Morten, giving him the care and love he had lacked as a child. She asked for nothing in return. For her, it was enough to know that Solveig and Morten were well. She loved her little family.

The house where they lived was a bit off the beaten path. There were no neighbors within walking distance, and Maja had to take the bus to the nearest town,

Knarvik, when she needed to shop.

"We can only afford one car on my salary, and I need it for work," Morten said when she suggested they buy a second car to make it easier for her to get around.

It had been ages since she had visited her old school friends. Her social life had been drastically reduced after she got married and had a child. She didn't get many visitors either. None of the people she knew had started families yet; they were still busy with studies, partying, and work.

Morten showed little understanding of her desire to meet other people.

"I need you. I need to know that you're here with Solveig when I'm at work, my own little family. It's just the three of us now; we don't need anyone else," he said, kissing her gently on the cheek.

Gradually, she stopped mentioning her friends. The love she had for Morten was a mix of understanding, pity, and respect. Her own needs faded with time.

Life went on, and Maja had plenty to do with Solveig and her daily tasks. She loved the little girl so much that her own life didn't seem to matter much. Maybe it was just as well that she didn't have visitors or seek out anyone; they would only be shocked by how she lived.

Only once had Maja asked Morten for help with the housework. The night before had been difficult, and after Morten left for work the next day, Solveig continued to be demanding. Maja was exhausted after months of sleepless nights. Not even during the day could she find a moment to rest. After dinner—salmon with roasted potatoes and vegetables—she asked if Morten could do the dishes. Solveig had finally calmed down, and Maja dreamed of a little time to herself on the couch.

What happened next was still a bit unclear to her. Without warning, she was pressed up against the wall by a strong hand around her throat. Morten's eyes flashed at her.

"You never ask me to do the dishes. That's your job. How useless are you?" he hissed before suddenly letting her go and storming out of the house.

The whole incident had happened so quickly, so unexpectedly, that Maja almost wondered if it had been real.

Later that evening, after they had gone to bed, Morten snuggled up to her, wanting to be held.

"I'm so sorry, little one, I was just completely overwhelmed; there's been a lot of stress at work lately. You know I love you, right?" he whispered in a thin voice.

A small seed took root in the pit of Maja's stomach. A small, dark lump, like dark clouds building on the horizon. But at that moment, with Morten lying in her arms, telling her how much she meant to him, she managed to push away the signs that had begun to reveal themselves.

Maja closes the diary. She is unsure if she has opened Pandora's box. Once she lets the memories in, they will be hard to stop. But maybe that's exactly what she needs? So much in her head is hidden in memory; truth and lies have blended into an indistinct mass.

"You know what, Doffen?" she says to the cat, who opens an eye when he hears his name. "We're going out for a bit. Fresh air clears the mind and lifts the mood, Grandpa always said, and now I'm saying it!"

From the closet, she grabs an extra pair of wool leggings, insulated overpants, a down jacket, a hat, a scarf, and mittens. Outside, the wind has died down, and the sun sends sharp rays through the cloud cover. Large snowdrifts cover the cabin, rendering it almost invisible in the landscape. Any random passersby would never discover this hidden refuge.

With the help of a shovel, Maja digs a small path down to the valley. She isn't worried about being seen. At this time of year, no one dares to venture into this area. She is completely alone.

Doffen stretches in the snow, slowly coming to life. The cold and the blanket of white covering the ground don't seem to bother him much. Maja throws small snowballs, which he playfully jumps up to catch.

"You look like a little snowman, or maybe a snow-cat," she laughs.

"Come on, let's see if we can make a snow figure—man or cat, it doesn't matter."

The cat isn't much help, doing everything he can to sabotage each attempt to roll a ball. Every time Maja gets well underway with what's supposed to be the snowman's body, the cat pounces and ruins it.

"Trickster cat, if you keep this up, you'll have to wait inside the cabin," she says, giving Doffen a stern look.

In the distance, Maja suddenly thinks she hears children's laughter—small voices giggling and laughing. Memories flood in: Solveig's first sledding trip with skis and a toboggan. Morten was there too, in the forest, sawing wood for the next winter.

"Self-sufficient with wood, that's something not many can boast of," he had said early one Saturday morning, two weeks after Solveig's first birthday. "Make some sandwiches and fill the thermos, and we'll take a trip to the forest, all three of us."

Happy that they were going to do something useful together, to go on an outing like a normal family, she packed the backpack and looked forward to a lovely day. But Morten's mood was unstable. Every day, Maja strained to ensure everything was in order. It became increasingly difficult; she never knew what might provoke an outburst.

Since the first time he had pinned her against the wall, he had found more and more things to complain about. The dinner was cold, the potatoes too hard, or she hadn't cleaned the floor well enough. Most often, she got an icy glare, but sometimes there was a fist to her side, or her back, or she was held tightly for a moment. And each time, he apologized. He showered her with tender words and soft kisses, and she, as always, forgave him. They needed each other, and Maja convinced herself that she had to try even harder to become a better mother and wife.

But this day in nature, she wanted to enjoy. They

were lucky; she knew that. The forest was right behind the house, and they didn't have to walk far to find a suitable spot for the day's outing. The fresh snow that had fallen the day before lay like a beautiful white blanket around the large spruce trees. She lifted Solveig out of the toboggan and whirled her around until they both gasped with laughter. Then she set her daughter down to teach her how to build a snowman.

"Look how nice it's turning out, with pinecones for eyes and a stick for a nose; it almost looks like a real person," she joked. "Maybe it'll become Frosty the Snowman, like in that cartoon you know."

Maja spread out the thick blanket she had brought, set out the sandwiches, and filled the mugs with coffee. Solveig got her cup of juice. Then Morten took a break from sawing, and they enjoyed a rare, pleasant moment together with their daughter. In the middle of chewing, Solveig exclaimed, "Daddy!" and pointed at the snow-man. She smiled so sweetly that Maja couldn't help but laugh along with her.

A darkness spread across Morten's face, and the next thing Maja felt was stinging cold against her cheek.

"So you think it's funny, do you? Are you making fun of me in front of my daughter? Who's the snowman now?" he shouted as he pressed her face hard against the snowman.

As suddenly as it began, he let go, got up, and kicked her hard in the stomach before picking up the chainsaw and walking away. Maja was left lying there, gasping for breath. The sound of Solveig's crying gave her the strength to crawl over to her daughter and comfort her. Some drops of blood fell on the snow, and she touched her face. The snowman's face, with its sticks and pine-cones, had scraped her skin.

Tears flow in torrents; the memories are too much to handle. Maja staggers back to the cabin. With Doffen under her arm, she closes the door, wanting to shut out all the bad thoughts, but she can't prevent a long breakdown, lying curled up on the floor for several hours. When she comes to, it's already dark outside. The flames in the small wood stove have died out, and she's shivering. Doffen lies next to her, purring loudly as she strokes his head.

"Imagine if everyone were like you, completely unconcerned about life. Loyal, too, loving me just as much, no matter how hopeless I am," she says quietly. "And I love you, my dear Doffen; you bring me back from the darkness every time."

After she gets the fire going, she heats a can of stew from her provisions. Then she sits down with her diary and writes about that fateful trip to the forest.

"Why didn't I leave him? All the warning signs should have made me react," she says, not expecting an answer from Doffen. "Weak, that's what I was. No willpower. Thought he would change if I just loved him enough."

The realization hits her hard. She had truly believed he would change if she did everything right and gave him all her love. How stupid could one be? How many times had she heard stories about other women being abused by their husbands? She had never understood why they stayed—how could they tolerate being treated like that?

Had she really become one of them, one of the countless women who couldn't take action?

The more she thinks about it, the more it dawns on her that this is exactly what happened. Trapped in a state of denial, she had degraded herself to a small fool who wasn't worthy of him, always searching for the slightest sign of love and attention.

After her grandfather passed away, she had been extremely vulnerable—alone in the world, with no one to love her. An easy target for a man like Morten.

"Oh my God, how classic—I've been so incredibly naive," she thinks aloud. "Talk about walking right into the trap with both feet."

Then she remembers the shadow. The dark side of her that emerged without her knowing why. Maybe it's true that she was the psychopath in the relationship. Her memories are so vague and unclear when it comes to the shadow. Almost as if it didn't happen, or like a slow-motion movie with her in the lead role. Could she have been completely wrong?

Tired and confused by all her thoughts, she throws the diary aside. What's the point of writing down a bunch of useless words if everything she remembers is just an illusion?

She puts a large log in the stove, blows out all the candles, checks that the door is locked, and goes to sleep in the bed beside Doffen. That night, she dreams of her grandfather.

Sitting by the bedside, her grandfather reads from what was her favorite book as a little girl, *Tom in the Wilderness.* The book is about a house cat, Tom, who is left behind at a mountain farm one summer when the people suddenly have to return home.

"Alone and abandoned, just like you, my Maja," he says in her dream. "But don't despair—one day, it will be you who is saved."

Ingvar

1945-1955

Life after Norway became a free nation has not been a bed of roses for Ingvar. The happiness that should have enveloped him never came. Instead, life became a battle against darkness and the struggle to survive. He often thinks it might have been better if he had died up there in the mountains.

In the first few days after his grandfather had helped him down from the mountain and brought him back to the farm, he was told nothing. All attempts to get answers about where his parents were and what had happened to Didrik were met with stern looks and admonitions that he needed to focus on getting well. The gunshot wound in his shoulder healed well, but he had contracted double pneumonia after his stay in the cold shelter.

It wasn't until several weeks after the liberation, on a beautiful and warm spring day, as they sat on the stone steps outside the front door of the house in Masfjordnes, that his grandmother finally told him the details.

Not long after he had enlisted in the Bjørn West Battalion, a serious incident occurred in Bergen. Early one morning, a fire broke out on the Dutch ship *Voorbode*, which was docked in Vågen for repairs.

The ship, fully loaded with ammunition and weapons, exploded, causing widespread devastation. Several houses were blown away, including the one where Ingvar's parents had just woken up, ready to start a new day. They didn't stand a chance and were killed instantly.

The grief hits Ingvar like a punch in the stomach. Both his parents are gone; he will never see them again. Didrik didn't survive either; he died from gunfire in the mountains while defending Norway and its freedom.

The guilt of having survived, along with the sorrow over everyone he has lost, weighs heavily on Ingvar for several months. He is paralyzed. His body doesn't function, and all he wants to do is lie in bed and stare at the ceiling. His grandparents leave him alone, not demanding anything from him. But around Christmas that year, his grandfather sits down next to him, and they have a long conversation.

"The war has treated us all harshly, and some have sacrificed more than others, but one thing is certain: we can't stop living," he says. "You are young and have your whole life ahead of you. I am convinced that both your parents and Didrik are very proud of you, and they would want you to have a good life. You must live in their honor. Never forget, but cherish what you have, and keep all the good memories in your heart."

The next morning, Ingvar wakes up with a slightly lighter heart. He decides to follow his grandfather's advice. Slowly but surely, he begins to return to life.

So does Norway. The post-war period, with new trade connections to the United States and the Marshall Plan, creates a foundation for economic growth. The country is united under the labor movement and the Labor Party, which aims to elevate all of Norway to a welfare state.

Changes are also underway in Masfjorden. Interest in power development in the mountains is growing. Enormous watercourses and waterfalls lie at their feet. It is a new era, and the people demand welfare, which requires large amounts of energy.

Ingvar is fortunate. After training as an engineer, he is hired by a municipal power company. He is finally ready to contribute to the industrialization of the country.

The mountains still call to him. Despite all the experiences during the war, both good and bad, it is here that he returns.

He hasn't forgotten the shelter, the cabin that saved his life when he needed a hiding place. What if another war comes? Or if Norway is occupied again? The thoughts of a secret hideout, a place where he could survive for many days, perhaps even weeks or years, start to take shape in his mind. His grandfather owns the land; they are both well acquainted with the area and have spent many hours hunting and fishing there.

Now he goes to his grandfather and shares his thoughts.

His grandfather is a calm man who doesn't get excited without good reason, but now he lights up and comes up with many ideas for carrying out the project.

"I am so proud of you, my boy. And this is something we can do together; it will be our secret," he says, moved.

It doesn't take long before they are well underway with the planning. The new construction road stretches further and further into the mountain wilderness; it has reached Stordalen, a beautiful valley surrounded by steep mountains with many gateways to the Stølsheimen nature area. This is good news for the two conspirators. To reach the shelter, they establish three different routes starting from the end of the construction road.

It is important that each path they use isn't too heavily trodden. They must ensure that they don't leave obvious marks in the landscape that could reveal where they are going. By alternating between different routes and never walking the same path twice, no one should be able to find the shelter.

Ingvar works on the creation of the power plant in Matre. He spends many hours on the construction road while overseeing work both at the fjord and the dam at Stordalsvatnet.

Through work, Ingvar finds refuge from all the sad memories. Most days, he manages to bury the pain and guilt that haunt him.

It was Didrik who died, not him. His parents, blown to pieces while he was far up in the mountains. These painful thoughts threaten to destroy him.

The plan for the secret hideout also helps to keep his

thoughts together. Every time he drives up into the mountains, he brings equipment to be transported further to the hiding place. No one asks questions; Ingvar has his own cabin, not far from the actual construction of the dam, where he has both storage space and the possibility to spend the night. On weekends, he picks up his grandfather, and together they make several trips back and forth between the cabin and the shelter.

In the beginning, there was a lot of material to transport. The first time they had returned to the shelter after the war ended, they had discovered a cave behind the simple plank building. This discovery gave the whole project a new perspective. It was no longer just about having a small, hidden hideout in a remote part of the mountain wilderness. The shelter was upgraded to a refuge—a bunker where one could be safe from both bombs and natural disasters. They decided that the shelter needed a dry and secure storage area, cast into the mountain.

Ingvar and his grandfather spent several months just transporting cement. Neither of them complained, even though the bags they carried back and forth on their strong backs were heavy. They found the stone and gravel they needed for the cement mix at the base of the scree by the shelter.

The project slowly but surely started to take shape. After two years of masonry and hauling, they completed what appeared to be a solid bunker, measuring three by four meters, with a ceiling height of two meters. A ventilation duct, which stretched several meters up through a crack in the mountain, ensured fresh air in the room.

They were fortunate to acquire the entrance door to the room through contacts and acquaintances from Marøy, an island out by the open sea, where the Germans had established a massive defense system during the war. Enormous bunkers and artillery were left abandoned after the war, and much of the material was sold to private individuals.

The steel door they acquired could withstand the pressure of several tons. It also weighed several hundred kilos. Transporting it up the mountain was a strenuous task for Ingvar and his grandfather. The mission had to be carried out in winter, after the first snow had fallen. Up and down steep slopes they went, on old wooden skis, with a homemade sled to which the door was strapped. Lifting the steel monster into place posed its own challenges, so ever the engineer, Ingvar designed a special winch for the purpose.

Many times they considered inviting some strong men from one of the work teams at the power company, but each time they concluded that it would be difficult to keep the shelter secret with too many people involved.

Indeed, a few curious people did wonder why they were spending so much time in the mountains, but the two made sure to always bring back some game from hunting and fishing on their trips so that there wouldn't be too much gossip. After the bunker itself was completed, they spent another three years building up the rest of the shelter.

Then, on a beautiful autumn day in late September 1955, they sat comfortably with their cups of coffee on one of the stone slabs leading to the secret entrance.

"This has been very rewarding," exclaimed his grandfather. "But what have we actually done?"

From his jacket pocket, he pulled out a well-worn pipe, which he carefully stuffed with tobacco. With practiced fingers, he lit a match and got the tobacco burning, slowly inhaling the smoke.

"Deep down, I hope we will never need this hideout, but now that it's made, it feels absolutely fantastic," replied Ingvar, moved. "I would never have made it through the last few years without you and this work, Grandpa."

In his mind, he saw his friend. He thought Didrik would have been proud of him. And his mother and father.

"Can we call it Didriksbu?" he asked quietly.

"You know what, I think that's an excellent choice. From now on, we will refer to the shelter as Didriksbu," his grandfather said solemnly, raising his coffee cup in a toast to mark the moment.

Maja

2016

For eight long years, Maja has lived without significant human contact. Isolated from the world, hidden away like an outcast, shielded from others' eyes. It's a self-imposed exile, a penance for her sins. If someone had told her ten years ago that she would be living alone in a remote mountain cabin, she wouldn't have believed them. It's too unreal. Who chooses something like that? The truth is, she'd had no choice. Circumstances forced her into exile.

Grief and pain awakened something within her she never thought existed—a near-sadistic satisfaction in subjecting herself to isolation. She believes she deserves this, and as the years pass, she embraces her punishment with something almost resembling joy.

But this summer, she wants to go out. Out into the world, if only for a little while. Not too far, but far enough for someone who hasn't been more than a few miles from home in years. She wants to follow the DNT trail that winds deeper into Stølsheimen, far beyond Vardadalsbu, the cabin where she has occasionally gone to buy food.

"Are you going to Voss?" she remembers the man asking, surprising her as she'd rummaged through canned goods at Vardadalsbu several years ago. The thought has crossed her mind from time to time—perhaps she should just take a trip to Voss?

The mountain village, just an hour's drive from Bergen, has always held a special place in her heart. It was there she learned to ski for the first time.

Her grandfather, who had grown up during World War II, wasn't impressed by what he called "modern ski nonsense."

"You have your cross-country skis, they must be good enough," he declared one day after a long discussion about the things she thought she needed.

"Everyone else has downhill skis. I'm the only one stuck with old-fashioned wooden ones. It's super embarrassing, Grandpa," she complained. But they agreed that she would get money to rent downhill skis when her school had a ski day at Voss.

Much to Grandpa's dismay, Maja became completely hooked on downhill skiing. It was as if she had waited her whole life for that day in seventh grade.

The feeling of floating several meters above the ground in the ski lift, being carried effortlessly to the top of the mountain, was indescribable. But what she loved most was racing straight down the steepest slopes. Fearlessly, she hurled herself down while the biggest boys in the class watched with terror in their eyes.

That Christmas, she received her own pair of downhill skis as a gift from her grandfather.

"I admit I've become an old-fashioned, out-of-touch

geezer," he laughed as she joyfully threw her arms around his neck.

"You're the world's best Grandpa, and you're not old and out of touch at all." Maja beamed. "If you were, I'd have sent you to a nursing home long ago."

Maja sets the good memories aside and finds her large mountain backpack. She has no plans to stay in the DNT cabins, so she packs both a tent and a sleeping bag. With a hoodie, sunglasses, and a cap, she hopes no one will recognize her. This time, she must be prepared to meet people.

It takes her a couple of hours on foot before she spots Vardadalsbu in the distance. Even before she sees the cabin, she hears voices—children playing and adults talking. Fortunately, the trail winds below the cabin along the river, a little out of sight from those staying there, so Maja manages to slip by unnoticed and continues up through a rocky pass. The trail is easy to follow, with most of the DNT markers—red Ts— painted clearly on rocks or cairns.

The sun is shining, it's quite warm, and the terrain is challenging. Stølsheimen is known for its steep mountains, deep ravines, rivers, and rocky paths. It's not an easy area to navigate, but Maja is accustomed to traveling off the beaten path.

As the sun sets, she decides to pitch her tent in a small valley surrounded by several waterfalls, with a small lake in the middle. She wades across a shallow river and finds a dry spot well away from the trail. She brings out her fishing rod, and after just a few casts, she gets a bite. The catch isn't large, but it's enough for a small evening meal cooked on the camp stove.

As evening turns to night, Maja crawls into her tent and sleeping bag. A small feeling of happiness washes over her—this trip has been a good choice and something she sorely needed.

The next morning, she quickly packs up the tent, stove, and her few belongings. The journey continues over yet another rocky pass, but also along quiet mountain lakes, where the scenery seems taken from a nineteenth-century painting.

Fortunately, there aren't many people on the trail, and Maja is delighted to experience new places. Several days pass like this until she approaches the DNT cabin Selhamar, which is idyllically situated a bit high up, offering a good view over the rugged landscape. She neither sees nor hears anyone else.

The weather has changed—rain and an icy wind have replaced the sun and warm temperatures. Although there's a high risk that other hikers might show up during the evening, Maja decides to spend the night in the cabin. The idea of sleeping in a tent in this weather is not appealing.

The cabin is large, with several bedrooms. She chooses one of the smaller ones but waits to unpack, in case a large group shows up and she needs to leave quickly.

It's a strange feeling to be in another cabin. Maja feels like an intruder. She wonders how things would have been if the girls were still alive. Would she have taken them to the mountains more often? Would they have grown to love the Masfjord mountains as much as she does?

After dinner and cleaning up, she settles into one of the armchairs with a book she found on a shelf.

Suddenly, the door opens, and in comes a young girl, soaking wet but with a big smile on her face.

"Hi, sorry to barge in like this, but I'm soaked from head to toe," she laughs, tossing her backpack in the middle of the floor.

Maja doesn't have time to react—she should have fled into her room, but she's so taken aback by the encounter with another person that she can't say a word.

"I'm so glad someone is here who has lit the fire. There's hope that everything will be dry by tomorrow," says the young girl.

Still without saying a word, Maja gets up and adds an extra log to the fire. There's something about the cheerful girl that captivates her, and she sits down and stares at her.

Then the girl extends her hand and introduces herself.

"My name is Malin, I'm from Bergen, but I'm currently studying in Oslo. I have two years left at the teacher's college. I can't wait to start teaching," she says with a laugh. "Sorry, I always get scolded for talking too much, but I've been alone on this trip for several days, so I can't keep quiet when I finally meet someone."

Maja smiles. She relaxes a little and thinks that the

girl should know that she herself hasn't spoken to anyone in years.

A bit rusty in her voice, she tells Malin that her name is Kari. She doesn't want to share anything more about herself, but Malin talks enough for both of them, so it doesn't seem to be a problem. It turns out that they've more or less followed the same route, but Malin has stayed in several of the DNT cabins that Maja has passed by.

Still a bit unsettled by the new acquaintance, Maja decides to share a little more about herself.

"I'm from Masfjorden. The mountains have always been my second home," she says, knowing there's more truth in those words than Malin will ever know.

"Masfjorden? That's cool! I did an internship at a middle school in Masfjordnes this spring. My god, what a place! I had to drive forever to and from work every day," Malin laughs. "Luckily, I got to rent an old house, but there was absolutely nothing to do in my free time there. But those mountains, though! One night, I slept under the open sky on Ådneburen—a fantastic experience."

A jolt goes through Maja when Malin mentions Masfjordnes, and she realizes she needs to be careful. The conversation has suddenly become too close, and she excuses herself rather brusquely and says good night. In the small room, she has to sit down to catch her breath. It's been a long time since she heard anyone talk about Masfjordnes, her grandfather, or her childhood home.

The next morning, she gets up at the crack of dawn. She wants to move on and put the encounter with Malin behind her. She skips breakfast, just grabbing some crispbread and soup packets for the next few days. She can't risk stopping at any more cabins; it's become too dangerous. From now on, she'll have to sleep in her tent out of sight of the trail.

That day, she can't concentrate on enjoying the hike or the landscape. Her thoughts keep drifting back to her childhood in Masfjordnes—the little log house, the barn, the shop by the quay, the beach with its smooth rocks, and, not least, the school where she had spent so many hours.

Morten never cared for Masfjordnes. When they got married, the houses she inherited from her grandfather were left empty and unused. She had suggested they could spend vacations there, but Morten always had other plans.

Maja scolds herself harshly and shakes off the heavy thoughts. "Now you need to focus on life here and now."

She has planned two more nights in the mountains before the descent to Voss. Her hope is to arrive early in the morning, stroll around the town, shop, eat some good food, and then start the return journey the same way she came.

As she gets closer to Voss, she encounters more and more hikers. A nod and a greeting here and there are thankfully enough, and Maja manages to avoid anything that might resemble the start of a conversation. The last night, she sleeps under the open sky on Slettafjellet. She's not sad, but it's a strange feeling to think about entering a town the next morning. Admittedly, not a big town, but it's Saturday, and the streets will surely be packed with tourists.

The starry sky above her is like a map. Maja locates the Big Dipper, the North Star, and Orion's Belt. And she sees her two favorite stars, lying close together, almost like twins. She has named them Solveig and Laura.

Many times, those two stars have given her strength after a breakdown. Or they've appeared in the sky after a tough period, calming her with their presence. Sometimes she's had long conversations with her daughters while lying in the heather, her gaze fixed on the glittering dots, thousands of light-years away, where only her imagination mattered.

The sun wakes her with its sharp rays early the next morning. The night has been good; in her dream, she was home in Masfjordnes with her two girls. She had been sitting on the well-worn stone steps outside the log house with a cup of coffee while the girls ran around in the grass with their pigtails and light summer dresses. The idyll was almost tangible; nothing could spoil the picture she had conjured in her dream.

After a quick breakfast, Maja begins the steep descent to Voss's town center. Now and then, a paraglider floats overhead; it's clear she's not the only one up early. Once she's down, she puts on her hoodie, cap, and sunglasses.

The first thing she does is buy a juicy hamburger with bacon, cheese, and fries at the local gas station. This is something she has dreamed of many times over the past years—food she hasn't eaten in forever. Soda has been scarce too, so a Pepsi Max tastes fantastic with the unhealthy meal. Sitting on a bench by Lake Vangsvatnet, Maja experiences a moment of pure happiness.

Afterward, she puts on her backpack and strolls along the lake. The sound of children playing football draws her attention. She had played football herself when she was in school, so when Solveig showed an interest in the same sport, she had encouraged her. The spring before the tragic incident, she had taken both girls to Voss Cup. She and Laura had stood on the sidelines cheering for Solveig, who, with her long blonde braids and oversized football jersey, had run around with the other kids. Still young, with no greater ambitions than maybe scoring a goal or two, but with an impressive determination to get the ball. Maja had been incredibly proud of her.

This Saturday morning, a beautiful summer day in June, it's not a football cup she hears, but a group of teenagers out playing on the field. Maja sits on a bench nearby and watches the game. A young girl with long, blonde hair stands out. She's light on her feet, easily dribbling the ball past the boys and kicking it hard straight into the goal. The other girls scream with joy and throw themselves at her.

"Sol, you're the best! None of the boys could ever beat you," one of the girls exclaims.

"We're going to win, thanks to you."

It's probably just a coincidence that the girl has the same nickname Maja used for her eldest daughter, but Maja flinches for a moment when she hears the name Sol.

How old are these teenagers? They look like they might be around fifteen or sixteen years old. Her Sol would have been about that age if she had grown up. Would she have continued with football, or would she have found other interests?

Maja can't take any more of her thoughts; she needs to tear herself away. As she gets up, she loses her balance for a moment before regaining it and moving on. Out of the corner of her eye, she sees some of the girls looking at her; they probably think she's a drunk.

She quickly heads for the nearest grocery store. There, she buys what she needs for the next few days in the mountains. Then she goes to a sports store, where she buys a pair of new, waterproof hiking boots. Socks, underwear, and a new set of wool thermal wear also find their way into her backpack. The few clothes she owns are well-worn, with years of patching and various repairs.

Maja takes a last farewell of Voss. It's bittersweet, but at the same time, she looks forward to returning to peace and quiet. All the noise from cars and people is almost too much; the years in isolation have really started to leave their mark.

Maja

2017

Back in the cabin, Maja realized that something within her had shifted after the long hike. A desire to see other people had begun to emerge. Soon, she started dreaming about returning to a different kind of life. How that might be possible, she didn't know. She decided to leave those dreams as just dreams and instead focus on planning more outings to places where she could satisfy her need to reconnect with humanity.

March arrives, and the mountain peaks glisten in the sunlight. The snow that came in winter never managed to cover the entire landscape, and now most of it has already melted. Rivers and waterfalls roar and thunder in their eternal battle to channel all the water down to the deep fjords.

Deep within the cold, dim cabin, Maja surveys her shelves of provisions, the canned goods gleaming faintly in the flicker of her lantern. Behind the thick iron door that Ingvar and his grandfather had painstakingly transported up to the mountains more than fifty years ago, the bunker remains as dry and intact as the day it was completed.

The food supply had been built up over several years and was meant to sustain two to three people for at least five years. Now, nearly nine years have passed.

Although Maja has been diligent in harvesting and gathering her own food, she has consumed quite a lot of the canned goods. Before long, they will run out. It's time for another expedition to civilization; she also needs essential dry goods.

If she hikes over the mountains down to the small village of Bjordal by the Sognefjord, it's not too far to carry the provisions back. But she has to be careful.

In small villages, everyone knows their neighbors, and word spreads quickly if a stranger shows up—especially one who walks down from the mountains, shops at the only store in town, and then heads back into the wilderness. Maja doesn't expect Bjordal to be any different from other small places.

She studies the map carefully and decides to try a route that is unlikely to be frequented by hikers so early in the season. From the closet, she retrieves the largest hiking backpack she owns, and early the next morning, she sets out on a new adventure.

Skis and a pulk work well in the open areas where the snow hasn't yet disappeared after the mild winter. At the snowline, she hides the skis and pulk behind some bushes. Now, only a few hours of steep terrain remain before she can walk the last few hundred meters to the store.

Down by the main road, she hides the backpack so that no one will suspect she's on a hiking trip. No one needs to know that she doesn't have a car parked somewhere; she must appear as a random passerby.

Fortunately, the road is empty, and Maja manages to

reach the paved main road unnoticed. The first houses she passes seem empty and abandoned. Everything is quiet. Outside the last house, just before she reaches the store, she sees an elderly man raking leaves in the garden. She quickly crosses to the other side of the road, pulls her hat down low over her ears, and nearly tiptoes past. The eyes watching her burn like hot coals on the back of her neck.

Inside the small convenience store, it's deserted. The shopkeeper is busy restocking and moves between the storeroom and the shelves. Maja quickly finds the sugar. If she buys too many packages, it could raise suspicion; no one makes jam at this time of year. Besides, they weigh quite a bit, and she has to carry them up steep, narrow mountain trails.

Five kilos of sugar, a few packs of oats, a pack of coarse flour, several cardboard boxes of beans and lentils, carrots, two packs of ground beef, some fruit, a few wheat rolls, five large bars of milk chocolate, and a Pepsi Max all fit into the shopping cart.

When she's ready to pay, the shopkeeper, a stout woman in her sixties, comes running over.

"Hello, there, sorry about the wait," she says with a big smile. "It's quiet at this time of day, so I try to get some tidying done in the storeroom. I don't remember seeing you in the village before—are you the one who moved into Sigmund's old house, perhaps? Someone told me that a couple was taking over the farm after the old man passed away," she says, peering curiously at Maja.

"No, I'm just passing through." Maja fumbled with the groceries, stuffing them into the flimsy plastic bags before rushing out of the store, away from the inquisitive woman.

She quickly passes the house where the elderly man was working in the garden. The man is nowhere to be seen, but when she glances at the house, she notices the curtains twitch behind the kitchen window.

Back at her backpack, she makes sure no cars are passing before crossing the road. Then she packs the groceries into her backpack and begins the steep climb up the gorge to where she's hidden her skis and pulk. Maja breathes a sigh of relief, satisfied with the day's expedition. She feels fairly confident that no one noticed her disappearing back into the mountains.

Morten didn't love the mountains the way Maja did. Whenever she suggested they buy a child carrier and take Solveig hiking, he dismissed the idea outright. There was always something that needed to be done at home, and he was meticulous about maintaining the house, both inside and out, which she appreciated. If something needed fixing, he would take care of it, but not without reminding her to stop breaking things. Of course, it was always her fault if a door started creaking, the oven stopped working, or a window wouldn't close properly.

Maja did everything she could to avoid his criticism, walking on eggshells around him, but no matter how careful she was, it always felt like he was waiting to find fault with her. His moods were unpredictable, and at times, his irrational behavior frightened her. But he loved her, and he was only trying to help her become a better version of herself, he repeatedly proclaimed. And Maja believed him, even after the serious incident when Solveig was barely three years old.

One morning, Morten told her he would be away for a few days; his job as a civil engineer at Statoil Mongstad required him to take an assignment in Stavanger.

"I'll be back on Monday at the usual time," he said, lifting Solveig up and giving her a kiss on the forehead. "You need to take care of Mommy while I'm gone, okay?"

"Are you taking the car?" Maja asked.

"Of course, you didn't think I was going to walk to Stavanger, did you?" he replied irritably. "What do you need the car for? Were you planning to go somewhere?"

"No, it's fine," she answered. "It just would have been nice for Solveig if we could have gone somewhere while you're away."

"You know I don't want you taking Solveig anywhere. Stay here. End of discussion," he said, giving her a stern look.

It was Friday, and Maja spent the day following her usual routines—washing dishes, tidying up, vacuuming, folding clothes, and cleaning the bathroom. Mostly occupied with her Lego blocks, Solveig was a quiet and observant child who didn't cause much fuss.

Maja loved her so much that it sometimes made her heart ache.

"Maybe we should go on a little hike, just you and me?" she whispered to her. "I know a beautiful spot, a secret place where the wind whispers through the treetops, the fish splash in the water, and the moss is as soft as cotton."

Maja made a sudden decision—a small expedition to the Masfjord Mountains was exactly what she needed. It had been years since she had gone anywhere; life with Morten and Solveig had demanded her full attention at home.

She packed a hiking backpack with a sleeping bag, a sleeping pad, the nostalgic camping stove she had inherited from her grandfather, a change of clothes for both of them, mosquito netting, and food and drink. The weather forecast promised sunshine, so she took the risk of leaving the tent behind. The bus stop was close to the main road, about a kilometer from the house. Solveig was ecstatic about the upcoming adventure, clapping her hands excitedly and running ahead. Maja laughed and called her back, the little girl beaming like a small sun, but obediently taking Maja's hand as they walked to the bus stop.

They had to change buses in Knarvik. The journey continued through long tunnels and narrow roads along Osterfjorden before the bus revved up the steep hills toward Dyrkolbotn. The landscape shifted from idyllic fjord scenery to high mountains with scattered, twisted birch trees, moss-covered rocks, and smooth mountainsides. Not long after, Maja and Solveig got off the bus.

They walked a couple of kilometers along an old construction road before they could start looking for the trail to the secret spot. Luckily, Solveig was a good walker; she didn't complain but stopped every time there was something to explore. A pinecone, some ants, several sheep behind a fence, a puddle—everything needed to be examined. The day was drawing to a close by the time they finally found the overgrown trail that only Maja knew about.

"At one time, this must have been a well-known place —it's too perfect for no one else to have discovered it," Maja thought to herself.

The trail wound steeply upward and had become quite overgrown. Solveig, with her small legs, was starting to get tired.

"Not much farther," Maja promised, lifting her over a root that had grown large across the path.

"Tired," Solveig said.

After about an hour, they arrived. The place was exactly as Maja remembered it. The large birch tree with its beautiful climbing branches stood tall and straight, just as it had the last time she was there. And the little pond with its perfect sandy beach still looked just as inviting. The water sparkled in the sunlight, calling them to it.

She set down her backpack and took off their shoes and socks. Together they waded into the lukewarm water. Solveig squealed with delight as she sank into the soft sand and the water washed over her toes. Maja took out her fishing rod. It didn't take long before she had caught two small trout, just enough for a dinner for one big and one small person. With practiced hands, she cleaned the fish, which were just right for their evening meal. After the meal, Maja found some pinecones. She stuck sticks into the pinecones, and voilà—she had made some sheep that her daughter eagerly played with.

The sun set, and Maja hung the mosquito netting over the branches of the large birch tree. She laid out the sleeping pads and sleeping bags. Solveig was completely exhausted from all the experiences and new impressions and fell asleep in an instant. Maja lay awake for a long time in the sleeping bag, gazing at the stars. How many times had she had such outings with her grandfather? The memories flooded back, and a tear welled up in the corner of her eye. Right now, she felt the sorrow and longing for her kind grandfather. A shooting star appeared—it was almost as if her grandfather was sending her a little encouragement—and she had a revelation.

She needed to show Morten this life, this side of her. If he only came with her once, she was sure he would see how perfect things could be together. She dreamed of lying here with Morten, looking at the stars, talking intimately about life, and making future plans. Maja clung to the desperate hope that if she could just show him this world—her world—he'd finally understand. Perhaps then, he'd love her the way she longed for, not with control but with tenderness.

Solveig woke early the next morning. She sat up in the sleeping bag and looked around cautiously, not quite sure where she was, until she spotted Maja and called out happily.

"More swimming," she said, pointing to the water.

Maja laughed and said yes, of course, a morning swim was the perfect way to start the day after a night under the open sky in the mountains. In just their underwear, they waded into the pool. The water was cool but provided a good start to the day, and they sat in the sun to dry while eating flatbread with brown cheese for breakfast.

Afterward, Maja packed up while Solveig tried to feed the pinecone sheep with grass. Although they felt a bit sad to leave the perfect spot, Maja was optimistic and excited to tell Morten about their experiences.

When Monday came, the house was perfectly tidy. Maja had put on a floral dress—Morten's favorite—and spent a long time making homemade meatballs with lingonberries she had picked herself, his favorite dish. Finally, she heard the car pull into the driveway. Not long after, they sat down at the dinner table, and Morten seemed pleased with the attention and the fact that she had made his favorite meal.

"So, what have you two been up to while missing me?" he asked with a small glint in his eye, looking at Solveig.

That's the last thing Maja remembered from that day.

The next morning, she woke up in a hospital bed at Haukeland University Hospital in Bergen.

A serious-looking doctor was standing over her, measuring her blood pressure.

"How are you feeling?" he asked gently. "Your husband brought you in last night with a concussion and several broken ribs."

Maja looked at him in confusion, trying to grasp what he was saying. The last thing she remembered was Solveig gobbling up meatballs, with brown sauce dripping down her cheeks.

"What happened? What am I doing here?" she asked, bewildered. Her head ached, and it hurt to speak.

"You fell down the basement stairs, don't you remember?" the doctor asked. "Your husband is very worried; he stayed with you all night. We sent him home this morning, told him to come back after he got a few hours of sleep."

The doctor examined her left eye, which was badly swollen, and her split lip.

"We've patched you up well. The swelling will go down, and you'll be just like before," he said, smiling at her.

After the doctor continued on his rounds, Maja fell asleep again. In her dreams, she saw two elves dancing in a dew-covered meadow in an enchanted forest. Suddenly, a dark shadow loomed in the dawning light.

Maja was jolted awake by Solveig's voice.

"Mama, Mama, you have to wake up. Solveig is here," she said in her soft, childlike voice.

She opened her eyes just in time to receive a wet kiss from her daughter before Morten intervened.

"You have to let Mama rest; she's hurt and needs peace," he said. Then he turned to Maja with a concerned look.

"How are you doing, my dear? That was quite a fall you had—you scared the life out of both of us," he said softly. "You remember that you fell down the stairs, don't you? A police officer is waiting to speak with you, so you need to tell them exactly what happened, how you tripped and hurt yourself."

Then he leaned over her and whispered so only she could hear, "You know it was an accident. If you say otherwise, you'll never see Solveig again."

A strong gust of wind jolts Maja back to reality. She shivers and pulls her hat further down over her ears.

"It must be the north wind picking up," she thinks. Not long after, she finds the sled and skis right where she had left them. She ties the backpack to the sled, sits on top of it, and eats a bun. Then she straps on her skis and starts the journey back to the cabin.

The memories of that fateful dinner after the hike with Solveig haunt her, as vivid as if it happened yesterday, and with them comes the reminder of everything she tried to forget. Even now, all these years later, she still doesn't clearly remember what happened, but lately, images of a fist and Solveig screaming have surfaced in the back of her mind. Along with them comes a vision of Morten standing over her, shouting.

"You're never doing that again. You'll do as I say. Dragging the little girl on a mountain hike? Filling her head with nonsense? Imagining that I'll do what you want? You'll never defy me again—I'll kill you both!"

The last few kilometers back to the cabin are exhausting. The wind picks up, and it starts to sleet. A sudden gust nearly knocks her off balance, and for a moment, panic seizes her—spending a night out here could be fatal. In these mountains, one misstep could send her tumbling into the abyss, lost to the storm. Even though she knows the mountains like the back of her hand, she is no match for the forces of nature. Finally, she spots the entrance to the scree slope in the distance.

Completely drained, she stumbles through the door, much to Doffen's surprise. The strain of the challenging journey and the flood of memories has overwhelmed her, and she falls into a restless sleep without eating or lighting the stove.

Ingvar

1955 – 1967

After Didriksbu was completed, the task of stocking provisions remained. Grandma, who had been enlisted as a co-conspirator, took the work of preserving and drying food very seriously.

"Whether the jars are stored here or way up in the mountains, it's all the same—they need to be eaten regardless," she said.

The war had left its mark. Feeding the family and ensuring that several of the more disadvantaged neighbors didn't starve, had been one of her responsibilities during the long occupation.

"What would we have done without you? No one will go hungry as long as you have a say in it," Grandpa chuckled from his easy chair in front of the fireplace.

Every weekend, as long as the weather permitted, Ingvar spent his time in the mountains. In the spring, before the snow melted, he was ready with skis and a sled, always carrying a few extra supplies in his pack to stock up the bunker.

It was a lonely life, but he didn't think much about it. So when some childhood friends invited him to a dance at the old fishing house in Masfjordnes, he wasn't very interested.

"Come on, it's time you found yourself a wife,"

teased his friend Sigurd. "You can't just roam around the mountains like a sheep.

You need to settle down and think about the future."

Ingvar knew he was right, but the thought of the opposite sex made him nervous. He had no idea how to talk to a girl.

"Alright, I'll go, but on one condition," he said. "I have to be home early. Grandpa needs help repairing the barn bridge."

Saturday morning, he regretted the whole thing. He would much rather spend the day hauling supplies up to Didriksbu. What on earth did he have to do at a country dance? But since he had promised to go, he had to keep his word, and when Sigurd picked him up, Ingvar had put on his finest shirt, which Grandma had ironed and starched to perfection. He had shaved and polished his shoes.

As they approached the fishing house, they heard cheerful tunes from a fiddle and accordion. The sound of people laughing and dancing was so loud, it almost lifted the roof. Sigurd guided him into the crowd of dancing young people and introduced him to the other friends.

Feeling a bit awkward, Ingvar stood by the wall, his gaze slowly moving over the crowd. Then he saw her. She was sitting a bit off to the side, sipping a glass of juice, with her light hair hanging loose over her shoulders. Ingvar couldn't take his eyes off her, and when she slowly turned and looked in his direction, he found himself staring into the bluest eyes he'd ever seen. Ingvar hadn't seen her in the village before, so he asked Sigurd for help.

"That's Kristine. She's one of the summer guests staying with the Kvingedal family, the ones who live in the yellow house not far from the pier, you know," Sigurd explained. "But I think she has a boyfriend in the city, so you can just forget about her," he added with a sly smile.

If there was one thing Ingvar couldn't do, it was forget Kristine. For the first time in his life, he realized he was in love. Over the next few weeks, he made frequent trips to the shop by the pier. Each time, he had to pass the Kvingedal house, always hoping to catch a glimpse of Kristine. Sometimes she sat outside the house with the other girls, who giggled when he walked by. Ingvar blushed every time and didn't dare to stop and talk.

One Friday evening, a few weeks later, he finally got the chance to talk to her. A group of young people had gathered by the freshly mown field belonging to Andreas, one of Sigurd's friends. Andreas's father had recently been to Bergen and brought back an exclusive record player.

Now, he was playing one tune after another, and when the classic hit *En Grønnmalt Benk* by the duo Gerd & Otto started playing through the speakers, Ingvar gathered his courage and sat down in the grass next to Kristine. His heart was pounding, and he was incredibly nervous. "It's now or never," he thought.

"My grandmother often sings that song. I know it by

heart," he said, trying to sound casual.

"I love that song. It's so romantic. One day, I'll have my own green-painted bench in the garden," she said dreamily.

"Then I'll build that bench for you, and I'll paint it in the finest shade of green you can imagine," Ingvar replied, blushing with embarrassment when he realized what he had just said.

To his great surprise, Kristine wasn't offended by his boldness but stayed and chatted with him. In the end, he got to walk her home, where he shyly asked if he could see her again.

For the rest of the summer, they spent every day together, and when the holiday was over and Kristine had to return to the city, Ingvar was heartbroken.

All autumn and winter, they exchanged letters. It turned out that Kristine didn't have a steady boyfriend in the city; it was just a childhood friend her parents thought she should marry. But after meeting Ingvar, she couldn't think of anyone else. Her parents had to accept that they couldn't force her, but they remained skeptical of this "farm boy," as they called him.

In the spring, Ingvar received a job assignment that sent him to Bergen. Each way took a whole day on the steamship *Lygra*, which had many stops along the route. Ingvar, who hadn't been to Bergen since his studies, was hesitant to return to his childhood haunts. But this time, someone was waiting for him. Still just as in love, he decided that she was the one he wanted to share his life with, and on his second day in Bergen, he visited a jeweler and bought an engagement ring.

Later that afternoon, he waited for her, sitting on a green-painted bench by Lille Lungegårdsvannet, just as nervous as the first time he had mustered the courage to talk to her.

Not long after, she appeared before him in a beautiful floral summer dress, white pumps, and a hand-knitted cardigan that matched the dress. She was stunning, and Ingvar felt his pulse race. Unable to take his eyes off her, Ingvar took her outstretched hand, then leaned in and gave her a gentle hug.

For the next hour, they sit and talk about everything and nothing, before Ingvar gathers the courage to take the small box from his pocket.

"I have something I need to ask you," he says cautiously. "Ever since I saw you that first night at the fishing house, I've only thought about you. Your beautiful blue eyes, your smile. All I want in life is to share it with you. I love you. Will you marry me?"

Kristine looks down for a moment, and Ingvar fears he's made a mistake.

"She's not interested in a country bumpkin like me," he thinks. Now she'll probably break up with him, and his life will be over.

Then she looks up at him with those big blue eyes.

"There's nothing I want more than to share my life with you," she says, tears streaming down her face.

Ingvar opens the box, slips the ring onto her finger, then leans in and kisses her gently on the lips. He has never been so happy in his entire life.

Back in Masfjordnes, he shares the good news with his grandparents. His grandmother quickly gets to her feet and gives him a warm hug. His grandfather smiles from ear to ear and goes to the liquor cabinet.

"What a joyous day! We must celebrate," he says, pouring a drink for all three of them. Then he raises his glass for a toast. "To all that has been, to all that will be, and to the happy couple. Cheers."

They waste no time in planning a late-summer wedding, and Kristine is set to move into the house Ingvar shares with his grandparents. With two living rooms, a kitchen, and three bedrooms, there's enough space, but the young couple wants to establish their own home. A plot on the farm is sectioned off, and a new, modern house with electricity, running water, and a toilet begins to take shape. A few months after the wedding, it becomes clear that they need to hurry with the new house—Kristine is pregnant and wants to give birth at home.

On May 8, 1957, the anniversary of the liberation, little Hans Arne is born, named after both of his grandfathers. Ingvar is overjoyed. Over the past few weeks, he has been focused on crafting a bench. But this is no ordinary bench. With the help of the local blacksmith, he has acquired exquisite wrought iron for the frame, which is painted black. The wood for the seat and backrest comes from their own forest. The bench, or rather the artwork, is painted in a deep, dark green. A small plaque with the words "Because I Love You" is placed on the backrest.

The little family soon settles into their new life. The years go by, and no more children come. Ingvar takes up the project of transporting provisions, gas canisters, firewood, and other survival supplies to Didriksbu again. Kristine is in on the secret and contributes as much as she can. When Hans Arne is old enough, they often spend several days in the mountains during the summer. They stay in the small cabin, make repairs, and ensure everything is in order.

In the 1960s, the construction road up to Stordalen is extended, making access to the cabin easier. Ingvar still works for the power company and has access to a snowmobile in winter. With a fully loaded trailer, there are no limits to how much he can bring up to Didriksbu. Slowly but surely, the supply depot is filled.

When Ingvar's grandmother doesn't come down from the attic after her daily afternoon nap on a cold January day in 1967, he goes upstairs to wake her. He finds her dead in bed.

"It's probably her heart," the doctor says when he comes to confirm the cause of death. "She passed away peacefully in her sleep."

Just a few months later, two days before Hans Arne's tenth birthday, his grandfather also passes away.

"Some people are so closely connected that when one of them dies, it doesn't take long before the other simply dies of grief," the doctor explains when he has to visit once again. The sorrow brings back old memories of the war, when Ingvar lost both his parents and his best friend, Didrik.

One early morning, he packs his bag and heads for the mountains, needing to be alone with his thoughts for a while. Kristine, who lost her parents a few years earlier, understands how he feels. They don't need to express words or emotions—they know each other's thoughts and understand the importance of giving the other space to process difficult events.

But when weeks pass without any word from Ingvar, Kristine packs her bag. She leaves Hans Arne with some good neighbors under the pretense of running an errand in town and might be gone for a week.

It's completely quiet when she approaches the cabin. A strong stench hits her as she opens the door. There, lying on the bunk, is Ingvar, lifeless. Her first thought is that he has taken his own life. Overcome with grief, she calls his name and shakes him. At first, there's no response, but then he opens his dull eyes and looks at her.

"Grandpa, is that really you? Have you come to take me home? I can't find Didrik. Can you fetch him for me?" he says in a slurred voice.

"It's me, Kristine, your wife," she replies. But Ingvar closes his eyes again and slumps back onto the pillow. She feels his forehead, which is burning hot, and quickly realizes that he's suffering from feverish delusions.

Kristine hurries to fetch water from the stream, starts

a fire in the stove, and warms the water. She gives Ingvar a good wash before changing the bed linens. Then she makes porridge with oats and blackcurrant syrup, which she feeds him. Afterward, she cleans and tidies the rest of the cabin.

When evening comes, she sits in the rocking chair by the bunk. Ingvar sleeps fitfully, and she alternates between cooling his forehead with a damp cloth and trying to get him to drink fluids. By dawn, he seems calmer, and she falls into a deep sleep in the chair.

She wakes up suddenly, shifts slightly in the unfamiliar sleeping position, and wonders for a moment where she is. Then she looks over at Ingvar and is met with a big smile.

"Is it really you, my dear wife, or am I seeing things?" he says in a hoarse voice.

"It's really me. I got worried when we didn't hear anything from you for so long," she replies, stroking his cheek. "I can't bear the thought of losing you too."

Kristine wipes away a tear, relieved that he is alive.

"I was actually considering ending it all. How can life ever be the same? There's so much sorrow and misery. I don't know how I can go through it all again," he says, looking at her with sad eyes. "For days, I wandered around. I visited the spot where Didrik was shot. Everything felt so meaningless. Back at the cabin, the fever knocked me out, and in my mind, I relived that week I lay here freezing before my grandfather found me."

He has never told her the whole story before, but now, once the words start flowing, he can't stop. Every detail

—from the first time he arrived at Bjørn West, to the gunshot wound, Didrik, the guilt, and everything he has carried with him for so many years—comes out. Afterward, he feels calmer than he has felt in a long time. Sharing his thoughts and everything he has experienced has lifted a burden from his heart.

"You know I love you more than anything in this world. Everything you've been through tears at my heart," she says, her voice choking up. "But life must go on—you have a wonderful boy who needs his father, and I need my husband."

Ingvar spends the next few days regaining his strength. In the evenings, they sit in front of the fireplace and talk. When Kristine and Ingvar finally pack up and start their journey back to civilization, they are closer than ever before.

Maja

2017

May brings with it an unusually warm westerly wind. The buds on the small dwarf birches that grow sporadically in the valley below the cabin burst earlier than expected. Even the wood anemones poke up from the ground long before they usually do. It feels like both spring and summer are in the air at the same time, and Maja feels the energy that comes with this season. She decides it's time for a good old-fashioned spring cleaning, something she hasn't bothered with before. Dust and dirt in the corners have become routine; it just hasn't seemed necessary to make everything sparkle. Neither she nor Doffen is particularly fussy about it.

Perhaps it's a reaction to all those years with Morten, who demanded that everything be perfect, never satisfied no matter how much she scrubbed and cleaned. Even after he had moved out, she had continued to keep everything in order. There was never a speck of dust on the coffee table in the living room or toothpaste residue in the bathroom sink.

But after her life was turned upside down, the need for perfection disappeared. Perhaps this is who she truly is? When she thinks back to the years with her grandfather, she can't recall either of them being obsessed with cleanliness. They had their regular tasks, but every Saturday, Maja would bring out the dust cloth and make an extra effort so that they wouldn't "let it get too bad," as her grandfather used to say.

Maja begins the spring cleaning inside the bunker. The room hasn't been used as living space, but the large storage area needs tidying up. Besides, it's time to check her inventory of how much food and other supplies she has left. If she's ever going to restock the room to the state it was in when she first moved in several years ago, she'll need to find new solutions.

The most important thing is access to a car so she can drive supplies as far up the mountain as possible, and also use the work shed as a temporary storage station.

Suddenly, a possible solution occurs to Maja. The property from her grandfather in Masfjorden is still registered in her name, but she has no idea what has happened to it. Most likely, the house stands unoccupied and empty, waiting for her to reappear, or the municipality may have taken it over if she has been declared dead.

There are no known heirs, at least none that she's aware of. It was just her and her grandfather—no aunts, uncles, cousins, or other close relatives.

If nothing has happened to the property since she disappeared, she imagines that her grandfather's old Opel is still in the garage. She had never been able to part with the car; there were too many memories tied to it.

It's not a bad plan, but it is risky. Maja has no guarantee that the car works, or that it will manage the steep drive up to Stordalen without breaking down. There's also the risk that someone will recognize it.

She finishes the inventory and makes a new list of everything she needs to replenish. The list seems as long as a bad year, and she realizes that she must implement the plan that has started to take shape in her mind. If she's going to survive the next few years in the cabin, she has no choice. The big spring cleaning is postponed until later. There are more important things to do now.

Early one morning at the end of May, she packs her backpack and sets off on foot towards Masfjordnes.

After walking all day and into the next, she reaches the outskirts of the farm just before the gray twilight hour. It's strange to be back after so many years. Maja moves cautiously toward the big house, not wanting to risk being discovered if anyone is there. But everything is quiet and peaceful—no cars in the yard, and every-thing looks untouched and overgrown.

She finds the key in the usual hiding place under one of the roof boards on the south side of the outhouse. Carefully, she inserts the key into the lock and turns it. A musty smell hits her. Slowly, she moves around the house, terrified that all the memories will flood in and ruin her mission. She quickly finds the car keys in their usual place in the colorful Iittala bowl, a gift from her to her grandfather many years ago.

Outside, it has grown dark. Fortunately, the property is some distance from the nearest neighbor, so she is not afraid that someone will pass by and discover her.

With practiced hands, she unhooks the padlock from the garage door and slips inside. A ceiling light bulb reveals the car, a blue Opel station wagon from 1987. Dust and debris have formed a thin layer over the paint, so Maja finds a brush to clean it up. She opens the hood and checks that there is enough oil. Then she retrieves the manual pump and refills the tires with air.

At the back of the garage, her grandfather had stored some containers of gasoline. Good old Grandpa, who always made sure to have reserves. Maja fills up the tank and gets into the car. Then she remembers the battery. "There can't possibly be any life left in it," she says to herself. She gets out of the car and opens the cabinet by the entrance door. Fortunately, she finds the charging cable.

"It's now or never," she says aloud and turns the key.

The Opel starts like clockwork on the first try, and Maja can't suppress a small cheer.

"I can't believe I'm so lucky," she exclaims. "Now it's time for an outing, just like the old days."

It's a wonderful feeling to zoom off in the old car. After only using her feet as transportation for several years, she feels euphoric and ecstatic.

It's been a long time since she felt such emotions, and she almost feels a little guilty. She has no right to be happy; she gave up that right a long time ago. She pushes away all the difficult thoughts and decides to enjoy this trip as much as possible.

Part two of the daring plan comes into effect. For someone who has been hiding from reality for nine years, it's not easy to suddenly appear in civilization again as if nothing has happened. There's a good chance someone will recognize her if she shows up at the local grocery store in Knarvik. She can't risk that. Besides, it's evening, and all the stores are closed. It might also look a bit strange if she fills a shopping cart with loads of canned goods and dry food; it might attract some extra glances and unwanted attention.

Maja decides to drive to other villages and visit several different grocery stores. The first thing she does is leave Masfjordnes and drive out of the municipality. It's one o'clock in the morning, and there is almost no traffic on the roads. She turns on the old cassette player and smiles to herself when Willie Nelson's classic *On the Road Again* streams out of the speakers. Her grandfather was a big fan of the country legend, and they always listened to Nelson when they drove.

"Imagine if you were here with me now, Grandpa. I wonder how you would feel. Would you condemn me, or would you love me no matter what?" she says into the air. She doesn't expect an answer, but the presence of her grandfather feels comforting and reassuring.

When she reaches Mo in Modalen, she parks the car on a side road, well hidden from the main road. After a quick meal of crispbread with Nugatti, she reclines the seat, pulls a wool blanket she had taken from the house over herself, and tries to get some sleep. But it's easier said than done.

The journey back to civilization stirs up so many memories, both good and bad. She thinks back to her time with Morten, the years before Laura was born. What really happened? So much is unclear in her mind, with many events she hasn't fully grasped. But one thing she'll never forget is the first time she woke up one morning at home in bed, with no memory of what had happened the night before.

Solveig had just turned four, and Morten had invited a colleague and his wife over. It wasn't often they socialized with friends or acquaintances, so this was a rare occasion.

"Per is a childhood friend of mine. He moved to eastern Norway many years ago, but now he's back and working in my department," Morten had explained. He had been in an unusually good mood for several weeks, ever since Per showed up. Maja had never heard of this Per before but was excited and looked forward to meeting one of Morten's friends.

She hadn't spoken to her childhood friends in years; they had stopped contacting her long ago. None of them got along particularly well with Morten, and he had long since convinced her that they weren't worth keeping around. They didn't care about her; only he did.

Saturday evening came, and Maja took extra care with her makeup and clothes. The house was freshly cleaned; she had even polished the windows and the furniture. Everything had to be perfect so Morten wouldn't be ashamed of a wife who didn't keep the house in order.

Solveig was still awake when she put on the potatoes to go with the venison roast. Morten wanted to show off their daughter, so Maja waited to put her to bed until the guests had greeted her. Not long after, the doorbell rang, and Morten went to open it. Cheerful voices filled the hallway as Per and his wife, Elise, entered the living room. A bit shy, Maja extended her hand and greeted Per.

"Now I see why you've been hiding her away, Morten," he said as he pulled her into a hug that lasted a bit too long. She smelled alcohol on his breath. Elise gave Maja a limp handshake while eyeing her with a scrutinizing look.

"You'll have to excuse my husband; he has a weakness for stay-at-home blondes," she said before turning to Morten with a fawning smile. "I need a GT, and right now. You'll take care of that, won't you?"

Then she noticed Solveig hiding behind Maja.

"And who is this little sweetheart? Let me see you," she said, pinching Solveig's cheek. "We don't have children, and we never will—it's way too much work, right, darling?" She turned to Per, who nodded in agreement.

Maja took Solveig to her bedroom. Even though the little girl was extra excited about having guests in the house, she laid down nicely and fell asleep after a short while. Maja sighed and gave her a quick kiss on the forehead before returning to Morten and the guests.

In the living room, the atmosphere was already quite lively. Elise was well settled on the sofa next to Morten, whom she clearly had taken a liking to. She openly flirted with him, constantly stroking his arm. Per sat in one of the chairs and didn't seem to mind his wife's behavior.

In the kitchen, Maja opened a bottle of red wine and took the roast out of the oven. She sliced it into thin pieces before arranging them on a platter with the vegetables. The potatoes were cooked, and the home-made game sauce was also ready, so she set everything on the dining table, which she had decorated with a freshly ironed white lace tablecloth, the best china, and candles and napkins in matching colors. Nothing had been left to chance. A bit nervous, she invited everyone to the table.

They sat down, and Morten poured the red wine. After two glasses, Maja felt a bit more cheerful and decided to enjoy the evening. It had been ages since she'd had more than one glass of wine, and even longer since she had partied with friends.

The guests praised the meal lavishly. After dessert and cognac, they returned to the living room, and Morten made gin and tonics for everyone. Per put on a playlist with funky music from Spotify, then pulled Maja up from the sofa and they danced, laughing loudly. Out of the corner of her eye, she noticed Elise, who now had one hand firmly placed on Morten's thigh. She was glued to him.

A twinge of jealousy hit Maja, but she let it pass. The music, the rhythm, the effects of the alcohol, and Per spinning her around the room were the last things she remembered from that night.

The next morning, she woke up with the taste of blood in her mouth. Her throat was dry, and she felt nauseous. The mattress beside her was empty, and the house was silent. Maja walked unsteadily to the bathroom. When she looked in the mirror, she was shocked. Her hair was a tangled mess, her makeup was smeared, and there was a large, swollen, red-and-blue stripe on one cheek. Her lip was split, and dried blood caked the corner of her mouth. She looked down at herself in confusion. Her body seemed intact, but several severe bruises on both arms were tender to the touch.

She went into the kitchen and was met with a horrible sight. Broken plates, leftovers from the venison roast, and red wine covered both the counter and the floor.

The living room didn't look much better. The furniture had been moved around, and several glasses were shattered on the coffee table. The floor was sticky from spilled alcohol.

"What on earth happened?" she asked herself. Her brain raced as she tried to piece together the previous evening, hour by hour. The last thing she remembered was the cheerful atmosphere—Per spinning her around the room, the feeling of joy. After that, everything went black.

Maja returned to the bathroom and freshened up as best she could. Then she took out a broom and dustpan and began to clean up. After a couple of hours, the house was somewhat back to normal, and she heard the front door open.

Solveig had come in and threw herself into Maja's arms.

"Mama, ouchie," she said, gently running a little finger over Maja's cheek.

"It's okay, sweetheart. It's just a scratch," Maja replied, struggling to hold back tears.

Morten didn't say a word as he walked past her into the kitchen and helped himself to the coffee she had made.

"You're useless. My God, you're actually crazy," Morten said, his back to her. "To embarrass me like that —what were you thinking?"

"What did I do? I honestly don't remember anything," she replied in a thin voice. "How did I get these bruises on my arms? And my face—it's a mess."

"Yeah, that's a convenient excuse, saying you don't remember anything. But let me tell you one thing: who I flirt with is none of your business! Your jealousy isn't charming," he snapped at her. "Slapping Elise like that —you completely lost it. Per had to hold you down while they waited for the taxi. And afterward, well, you just went nuts. You smashed everything you could get your hands on. That black eye is your own fault—it was self-defense."

That first horrible episode blurred together with other similar ones. Maja would wake up to shattered mirrors, curtains torn down, and ornaments destroyed. Every time, she had a bruise somewhere on her body, a black eye, or a split lip. And every time, Maja remembered nothing. But whenever Morten had a bruise, too, the story was always the same: she had been pathologically jealous over him flirting with Elise, and she suspected he was seeing her in secret. They had argued, and she had "snapped," as he put it. More than once, he had to restrain her to calm her down. All she remembered was having a glass or two of wine—never enough to get drunk.

"I'm ashamed of you—who knows what you might do next?" he sneered at her. "I'm never inviting friends over again."

After a few hours of sleep, Maja wakes up stiff and sore, sitting in her grandfather's car. At first, she doesn't understand anything—where is she? Suddenly, she remembers everything that happened the day before. The car, the journey, the expedition. The sense of adventure returns as Maja straightens the seatback and turns the ignition. Once again, the Opel doesn't protest but starts up on command.

Today, she's going shopping. Money is not an issue. The day she fled to the mountains, she withdrew ten thousand kroner from her account. Besides this, she had found around one hundred thousand kroner hidden in a small safe in the bunker.

Her plan is to drive to Voss via the narrow, winding roads toward Dale. The first stop is the grocery store there. Dressed in a hoodie, cap, and sunglasses, she quickly completes her errand. Then, she stops by a gas station to buy some fuel canisters. She repeats the same process at four more stores and two gas stations in Voss before visiting a few sports stores to buy more woolen underwear, hiking boots, a jacket, and pants.

Satisfied with herself, she returns to the car, which is now quite full of supplies. She feels confident that no one has noticed her. Back in Mo, she just manages to catch the small local shop before it closes. Here, she treats herself to some fresh food, like meat patties, chicken, yogurt, and baked goods. She sits on a bench by the pier and enjoys a delicious chocolate croissant and a Pepsi Max.

As darkness begins to fall, she starts the steep ascent past the waterfall and continues along the construction road toward Stølsvatnet. Almost at the end of the lake, she encounters an oncoming car. The road is narrow, and she has to pull to the side to let it pass. Slowly, the car inches toward her but doesn't drive by. The driver signals for her to open the window. Maja grabs the window crank and makes a small opening at the top.

"There are some large rocks that have fallen onto the road further ahead. They're hard to see in the dark, so be careful," says a friendly man who looks to be in his fifties. "If you're planning to camp, I wouldn't pitch a tent there. You never know if more might come tumbling down the mountainside," he adds.

"Thank you, I'll be careful," Maja replies before quickly rolling up the window and driving on with her heart in her throat.

After a short distance, she sees what he meant. Large rocks have made the road almost impassable, and the old car takes a beating. She carefully maneuvers around them, and soon after, she reaches the end of the construction road. She has been here with her grandfather several times. As one of the landowners in the mountains, he had received permission many years ago to keep a work shed by the lake.

Fortunately, the shed is still standing, though the years have not been kind to it. The paint is peeling in several places, and some of the wallboards need replacing. But Maja has no time to lose; the risk of being discovered by curious hikers or other landowners is real. She backs the car as close to the shed as possible, then goes back and forth until the car is empty and the shed has resumed its original purpose.

No more cars appear, and Maja closes and locks up before driving back the same way, heading toward Masfjordnes. Back at her childhood home, she parks the car in the barn, then resolutely walks to the main house. She unlocks the door and goes to sleep in her old room. Completely exhausted from the day's efforts, she falls asleep as soon as her head hits the pillow.

Maja

2018

Something unusual is happening in the Stølsheimen mountains this winter. A place that is typically quiet and free from activity during the coldest months has been unusually busy. Throughout the autumn, cabins and equipment have been transported up there. Large trucks have navigated the steep, barely passable roads—roads meant for regular cars, not heavy vehicles.

Nearly every day for several weeks, the sound of helicopter rotors has filled the air over Stordalsvatnet. Helicopters shuttle up and down from the fjord, carrying equipment suspended beneath them.

A major maintenance operation is underway. Preparations started in the fall with the draining of several large mountain lakes to allow access to the dam shafts. The once-idyllic lakes have lost their charm, now resembling giant craters, much to the dismay of tourists and cabin owners.

Up in Didriksbu, Maja and Doffen are staying indoors. The temperature has dropped well below freezing and remained there for weeks. Despite the clear, sunny weather, the biting cold wind makes it dangerous for both people and animals to be outside. Time passes slowly in the small cabin, far removed from everything most people take for granted.

There are hours, days, and even weeks when Maja struggles to cope with how her life has turned out. A lingering sense of loss stays with her, especially when she thinks about her grandfather and her two daughters. At times, she even misses Morten—the man who had once been her great love, her only love. Even though he left her, calling her a "psychopath," she remembers the sweet boy who kissed her outside the dance hall, back when everything was innocent and beautiful.

When she became pregnant with Laura, Morten seemed to return to his kind, caring self. The morning sickness wasn't as severe as it had been with Solveig, and Morten asked her every day how she was feeling. He made sure she ate properly and took her vitamins.

"This time, it's a boy. I'm sure of it," he said smiling one night as they lay in bed. "A little Morten Junior to carry on the family name."

Maja didn't argue. She hoped for a boy as well. Perhaps that would finally make Morten happy with her. She had certainly tried to meet his expectations. As a stay-at-home, pregnant mother of a small child, she kept the house immaculate, baked all the bread herself, and made sure there was a healthy, home-cooked dinner on the table every day. All she wanted was to give her children a good, stable upbringing, with a mother who was always present.

"If it's a boy, I'd like to name him Ingvar, after my Grandpa," she said. "I think he would have liked that." Morten turned towards her, his eyes flashing briefly.

Then, he gently stroked her hair.

"No, his name will be Lars. Ingvar is too old-fashioned. It has to be Lars, after my grandfather. No discussion—the father's side should carry on the name," he said firmly.

Maja knew there was no point in arguing. She hoped he might accept Ingvar as a middle name, but that was a conversation for after the baby's birth. Right now, she didn't want to stir up any tension.

A few days before her due date, Maja woke up in the middle of the night with familiar pains. Labor had started. Knowing it could take hours, she calmly got up and began packing for the hospital—a few extra clothes, toiletries, and her phone. If everything went smoothly, she'd be home the next day.

In the early morning, Morten woke up to find her fully dressed in the hallway with her bag.

"I think little Lars is ready to meet us," she said as a contraction made her double over. "They're still a few minutes apart, but it's getting closer."

Morten fetched Solveig, who immediately sensed that something was different—it was Dad waking her up, not Mom.

"Come on, you need to be a good girl. We're taking Mom to the hospital, and you're going to get a little brother," he said.

Hours later, Maja sat in the hospital bed, exhausted but content, holding baby Laura in her arms. She looked forward to Morten and Solveig visiting. When they arrived, Solveig climbed onto the bed, wide-eyed with wonder at the newborn. Laura opened her eyes just then and gazed at her sister, who gently stroked her cheek. In that moment, a bond was formed, and Solveig took on the role of big sister with seriousness and pride.

"Don't you want to hold her?" Maja asked Morten, who stood at the foot of the bed.

He walked over, glanced at the baby, and then leaned in, whispering just loud enough for her to hear.

"You're completely useless. It was supposed to be a boy," he said coldly, before picking up Solveig and walking out.

The next day, he came to take them home. Maja was dropped off without a word, left alone with the two children. Later that night, Morten stumbled into the bedroom, drunk.

"Useless woman. Can't even give me a son," he slurred, delivering a hard punch to her stomach. Maja collapsed to the floor as he continued hitting and kicking her. When he was done, he went to the living room and passed out on the couch.

The commotion woke the baby. Despite the searing pain, Maja managed to lift Laura and nurse her. Thankfully, she fell asleep quickly. Maja laid her in the bed and retreated to the bathroom. Her body was battered, and she was bleeding heavily. She changed into clean underwear and put on two large hospital pads. Crawling back to bed, she curled up next to Laura and drifted into a fitful sleep.

The next morning, she could barely move. The pain in her body and lower abdomen was unbearable.

She reached for the phone and dialed 113.

It didn't take long for the ambulance to arrive. Morten played the role of the concerned husband well.

"My goodness, what happened? Did you fall again? You should have woken me up; you don't have to do everything yourself," he said, ensuring the doctor examining her understood his concern.

"We need to take you to the hospital; you've recently given birth, and I'm worried about the bleeding," the doctor said. "The baby can come along. A nurse will take care of her and ensure you can breastfeed."

Once they reached the hospital, Maja was rushed into surgery. When she woke from the anesthesia, the doctor was by her side.

"That must have been a nasty fall, judging by all the bruises. Is there something you'd like to tell me?" he asked seriously.

"I'm so clumsy; it was my fault. I wasn't careful enough," she replied, looking away. The threat from Morten after her last "fall" still loomed in the back of her mind.

"Alright, that's up to you, but if you change your mind, let me know," the doctor said. "We've done what we can, but there's a high chance you won't be able to have more children."

Maja froze. How was she supposed to give Morten a son now? He would never forgive her for this.

"Please, don't tell my husband anything; he desperately wants a son," she pleaded.

"Don't worry, this stays between us. You decide what

to tell him. Feel free to contact me if you have any questions," the doctor said, giving her a small smile before continuing his rounds.

A few days later, she was well enough to go home. Solveig was overjoyed to have both her mother and little sister back. Morten held her close, unsure how to make up for what had happened.

"I'm so sorry. I was disappointed it wasn't a boy, and then I ended up drinking with some friends," he said, choking back tears. "It will never happen again, I promise. We can try for a boy next time."

Life soon returned to its usual rhythm. Maja enjoyed her time at home with the two sweet girls, tending to the house and ensuring there was dinner on the table when Morten came home. But she kept the big secret to herself.

Due to the increased activity in the mountains, Maja had to be extra cautious whenever she went down to the cabin to fetch supplies from the stockpile she had built after last summer's daring drive. Large vehicles, work trailers, and materials were positioned just meters away, increasing the risk of being spotted. Fortunately, the helicopters hadn't flown directly over the cabin, but their constant hum was never far from her valley.

To pass the long winter months, Maja had continued her diary project. She wove daily notes from her current life, filled with routines, together with fragments from her life with Morten and the girls.

Her goal was to piece together the events she still

didn't fully understand or remember.

Was she really a psychopath? She thought she must be. Normal people don't vandalize cars or set their ex's house on fire with the kids inside. All the episodes of pathological jealousy, violence, and aggression surely pointed to an unstable woman with a personality disorder. And what about the doctor who had given her the diagnosis?

The humiliation had been unbearable when Morten took her to Sandviken Hospital, the psychiatric ward, for a consultation. Just days earlier, she'd had one of her "episodes," as Morten called them. She couldn't remember much, but the small cut on Morten's forehead and the broken plates in the living room served as evidence of a heated argument. Maja had bruises on her upper arms, the result of Morten restraining her until she calmed down.

Sitting quietly next to Morten in the doctor's office, she listened as he described, his voice thick with emotion, the despair he felt over her behavior. He expressed concern for the girls and confessed he barely dared to leave them to go to work.

The doctor, an older man with glasses and a gray beard, had listened seriously before lecturing on the warning signs of psychosis.

"The jealousy, lack of impulse control, aggressive outbursts, and refusal to take responsibility—these are clear indicators of severe psychopathic traits," he said to Morten. "Hospitalization may be necessary if things don't improve, but we could try medication first."

Maja had no strength to resist. She sat quietly, like a helpless child, allowing the doctor and Morten to decide what was best for her.

She pauses her writing for a moment. It's hard to relive the complete helplessness she felt in that office. No matter what she said, it wouldn't have mattered—the doctor had taken Morten seriously and viewed her as a severe case.

"What do you think, Doffen? Am I a psychopath, a danger to society, condemned to a life in exile?" she asks, glancing over at the cat, who doesn't bother to react.

Maja gets up from the table, pulls on her warm suit, hat, scarf, and mittens. Fresh air—that's what she needs now. Outside, it's freezing but calm. She straps on her skis and slowly climbs the steep terrain where the cabin is hidden. As she reaches the first plateau, she leaves the shadows behind, and the sun's rays create a sparkling carpet of snow. The beautiful landscape fills her heart. The soft swishing of her skis echoes in the stillness, and the tracks she leaves behind are the only signs of human presence in the untouched wilderness.

Approaching the popular mountain peak Geitenakken, Maja hears the sound of a helicopter. There's nowhere to hide; in the open white landscape, she's completely exposed. The sound grows louder. Maja steers her skis toward a large rock where the snow hasn't settled. She ducks behind it just as the helicopter comes into view.

It flies low, but if they spot her or her tracks, she hopes they'll assume she's one of the cabin owners daring to venture out in the cold. The hum of the helicopter fades as it disappears over the horizon. Her pulse returns to normal, and she continues her ski trip.

The view from the top of the mountain is breathtaking. Snow-covered peaks stretch in every direction, with deep valleys, fjords, and frozen lakes as far as the eye can see. Down near the large dam, where Ikjefjorden comes into view, something catches her attention—something that doesn't belong on the small beach so popular in summer. If she looks closely between the large ice floes, she can make out the outline of what seems to be a vehicle. Sunlight reflects off the metal, casting sharp rays that seem to call out, "Hey, I'm here, come and find me."

But Maja is too far away to see clearly. She takes a few deep breaths, enjoying the feeling of satisfaction that comes with the intense silence only found on a mountaintop, far from civilization.

Knut

2018

The file that lands on Chief Inspector Knut Langholm's desk one early morning in September doesn't immediately catch his attention. In fact, several days pass before he finds time to open it, as he is overwhelmed with work.

The report isn't long, but the file contains many photos. A car was pulled out of one of the large lakes in Stølsheimen earlier that spring, and no one knows how it ended up there.

. Knut's first thought is that some teenagers might have stolen the car, joyridden in the mountains, and then panicked, dumping it in the lake. The car shows signs of having been submerged for many years. The license plate is unreadable, but it's a blue 1998 Toyota Corolla wagon. Fortunately, the skilled technicians managed to find the chassis number.

His first step is to contact the Norwegian Public Roads Administration, which promises to assign someone to the case. They warn him that locating old chassis numbers can be a lengthy process, as it requires manual searching.

The photos of the car don't provide any immediate clues, but he recognizes the landscape—it's a place where he's camped several times.

He hasn't had time for any trips to the mountains this summer. The few weeks he had off from his job as chief inspector at the Nordhordland police station, he spent replacing roof tiles and siding on his parents' old house. It was work he enjoyed, but he missed the peace and solitude the mountains offered.

The report accompanying the photos is sparse. The technicians thoroughly searched the car for clues but found only a few items: a child's car seat, some textiles of unknown origin, a wallet with unreadable credit cards, and a bag with size 32 football shoes. It appears to be a family car. And family cars don't just end up in mountain lakes. Most likely, the car had been stolen.

A quick search in the missing cars database yields no results. However, something else catches his attention —a picture of a similar car in a newspaper article from the local paper *Strilen*, dated July 8, 2008.

"Mother of young children missing without a trace," the headline reads. He keeps reading.

"The 28-year-old Maja Sandnes disappeared without a trace from her home more than three weeks ago. The woman, a resident of Alver municipality, is divorced and stays at home with her two daughters, aged 2 and 8. The daughters were on holiday with their father when the woman went missing. Evidence found at the home has led police to believe that something criminal may have occurred. 'The police have opened a case,' says police officer Oddmund Sletten of the Nordhordland police station to *Strilen*. Although the police are withholding details, the newspaper understands the findings may be connected to the fact that the woman's ex-husband's house burned to the ground on the same day she disappeared. The police are seeking tips from the public."

Knut feels a jolt. He remembers this case well. As a young, newly trained officer, he had once knocked on Maja Sandnes's door early one morning, the year before she disappeared. The ex-husband had accused her of vandalism, if he recalls correctly. A little girl had opened the door. Maja denied the accusations calmly and convincingly, and Knut had no doubt—the sweet woman with two adorable girls couldn't have been behind the ugly allegations.

Back at the office, he had reviewed the case. It turned out that the ex-husband had accused her of various things, but he couldn't convince anyone. The file also contained pictures of Maja from a previous hospital stay. She hadn't reported her husband back then, instead claiming she had fallen down the basement stairs. Due to a lack of evidence and several indications that the ex-husband could have staged the vandalism, Knut had closed the case.

Maja's car disappeared when she did. Could it be the one that has now surfaced in a mountain lake several miles from her home?

A few days later, he receives a call from the Roads Administration confirming his suspicion. The car is registered to a Maja Sandnes, with an address in Alver municipality.

"Damn," he mutters to himself. "Are we finally going to solve that mystery?"

Together with police officer Maren Hosteland, Knut visits the scrapyard in Kjevikdalen, where the car is being held pending further investigation. When the car was pulled from the water, it had been covered in mud and algae. After the initial forensic examination, it was cleaned to make it easier to inspect all the nooks and crannies. But nothing else was found—the car was empty.

Knut examines what remains of the car and notices that the driver's side window is open.

"Can you check with the recovery team if the window was open when they pulled it out?" he asks Maren, who nods and pulls out her phone.

After a brief conversation, she turns to Knut.

"Yes, they confirm it was open. What does that mean?" she wonders.

Maren is a recent graduate from the police academy and has been working at the Nordhordland police station for only three months. As her supervisor, Knut has taken it upon himself to mentor her, something he enjoys. The young woman is cheerful and easygoing but takes her job very seriously. They make a good team.

"Since the car belongs to a missing person and was found several meters deep in a mountain lake, I had expected we might find remains," he replies gravely. "But with the window open, it could suggest she tried to get out but didn't make it to the surface before drowning."

"Should we search the lake for her?" Maren suggests. "Should I call the dive team?"

"No, it's been too long; there's nothing left to find. Besides, the lake is large, and there are several waterfalls where remains could have disappeared," he says. "I think we should focus on notifying the family instead. Can you find out where they live?"

Not long after, they are on their way to the same address where Knut had once questioned Maja about the vandalism accusations. "It must be about ten years ago," he thinks. Even now, he is convinced something wasn't right back then.

As they pull into the driveway, he notes how well-kept both the house and yard are.

"Not much chaos here. You wouldn't think they had four kids; it's way too tidy," Maren remarks, noticing the same thing. "You should see our place. My mom gave up a long time ago," she adds with a laugh. She still lives with her parents and two younger siblings.

They park in the driveway, walk up to the front door, and ring the bell. After a moment, a woman with long blonde hair opens the door. Her gaze is distant, and she seems tired. Knut estimates she must be around thirty.

"Hi, are you Kjersti?" he asks.

"Yes, how can I help you?" she replies, looking anxious.

"Is your husband home?" he asks.

"We're having dinner right now. Could you come back later?" she says cautiously.

"This won't take long. We need to speak with both of

you," he says, stepping past her into the house. Maren follows, and Kjersti sighs as she closes the door.

In the kitchen, Morten has risen from the table, visibly irritated but holding it in. Four children, two girls and two boys, sit around the table, quietly observing the officers.

"How can we help you?" Morten asks, gesturing them into the living room.

"Something has come up," Knut begins. "A car was found in a mountain lake in Stølsheimen. The chassis number shows that it belonged to your ex-wife, Maja Sandnes."

The silence that follows is thick. No one speaks. A small gasp comes from the kitchen.

"In the car, we found a wallet containing credit cards and a driver's license. There is reason to believe she may have died, though no remains were found. The car has been submerged for many years."

"So that's where she ended up? She set fire to my house, that's what she did. Did you know that, officer?" Morten says sarcastically. "A murderer, that's what she is. If we hadn't had an early flight to Gran Canaria that night, we'd all be dead."

Kjersti remains completely silent, a small tear rolling down her cheek.

"What happens next?" she asks.

"That's up to the judge. Most likely, she will be declared dead," Knut explains. "If you have any questions or information that might shed light on the case, please contact me or my colleague," he adds.

Back in the car, Knut sighs heavily.

"I've seen far too many men like him. Did you notice how nervous his wife was?" he says to Maren. "Behind that seemingly perfect facade, there are many secrets. You can be sure of that."

Knut starts the car and is about to shift into first gear when the front door opens, and the oldest daughter runs towards them. He rolls down the window.

"Is it true? Is she really dead? Couldn't she have disappeared somewhere else? Maybe she was kidnapped or something," she asks desperately.

"It's very unlikely. I'm sorry, but your mother is most likely dead," Knut replies with a sad smile.

"Here," she says, handing him a small note. "Call me if something comes up. I'm convinced she's alive."

Knut looks at the note. It has a mobile number and the name Solveig written on it.

Back at the office, Knut can't find peace. The missing person case is bothering him. There's something he's overlooking, but what could it be? After a quick search in the police's digital archives, he finds the report from the fire.

Early that morning, while most people were still asleep, a passerby noticed smoke coming from the basement of a house in the neighborhood. By the time the fire department arrived, the house was engulfed in flames. No one could account for the occupants. Everything pointed to them having perished in the fire. It wasn't until late in the evening that the fire crew could safely search the ruins. Fortunately, they found only charred furniture and scorched appliances.

The next morning, the police received a call from an angry man claiming to own the house. The man identified himself as Morten Skogen and said that he and his partner, Kjersti, were on vacation with his two children from a previous marriage.

"The fire was arson, and I know who did it," he claimed. "My ex-wife has harassed us for a long time. No one has taken me seriously, but this time she's gone too far. This is attempted murder."

Based on this information, the police sent a patrol to Maja's home. There, they found the house locked, the car gone, and she wasn't answering her phone. After trying to reach her for several days, the police decided to break in.

What they found raised suspicions of foul play: an empty gas can, rubber boots with burn marks, clothes strewn across the bathroom floor, and a strong smell of smoke and gasoline. They also found several empty wine bottles, broken wine glasses, red wine stains on the sofa and coffee table, and an empty lighter.

These findings couldn't prove Maja had started the fire, but they didn't rule out that something had happened to her either. Maja was listed as a person of interest, but no one openly accused her, although her ex-husband remained certain of her guilt.

It wasn't until a year later that the fire inspectors' report came back. To everyone's surprise, they concluded the fire was most likely not arson. The exact cause was difficult to determine, but they suspected a fault in the fuse box in the basement, close to where a witness had seen smoke. A melted gas can was found near the basement entrance, which raised suspicion, but the lack of evidence made the case difficult, causing it to eventually go cold.

However, the big question remained: What had happened to Maja? Could her ex-husband have done something to her? He had been questioned several times by the police, and each time, he accused her of being pathologically jealous and violent. In his eyes, there was no doubt she had tried to kill them all, including her own children.

Kjersti provided Morten with an alibi for both the evening before and the night in question. Since they had left for Flesland to catch an early flight to Gran Canaria at 4 a.m., it would have been very difficult for Morten to have enough time to get rid of Maja.

Could the fire have been Maja's doing? It's rare for a mother to harm her own children, and Knut has a hard time believing she could have done something like that. Perhaps she acted under the influence, woke up the next morning, felt guilty, and decided to drown herself in Stølsvatnet?

Knut remains skeptical. He has always been told he is a good judge of character. The impression he had of Maja when he and his colleague visited her home after her ex-husband's accusations tells him she wasn't the type to harm her own children. The way she held her youngest daughter and gently stroked the hair of her eldest was loving and didn't suggest a mother who wanted to hurt her kids. But the most crucial piece of evidence for Knut is the hospital report. He has handled enough domestic violence cases to recognize the signs. He knows how women often hide abuse, especially when children are involved.

The fact that Maja claimed she had fallen down the basement stairs was a clear indication—she was protecting her children. Abusers manipulate such women into believing that if they speak up, they'll lose their children. The police often feel powerless in these cases.

Now, it's up to the judge to decide what happens next. There's only circumstantial evidence and too little proof to treat the disappearance as a murder case. Knut himself hasn't recommended searching the lake, doubting they'd find anything—it's been too long. But if the family requests it or the judge deems it a reasonable use of resources, he'll support it. From experience, though, he expects the case will be closed, and Maja will be declared dead.

Later that fall, Knut gets a few unexpected days off. The weather forecast promises sunshine and beautiful conditions, so he decides to pack his bag and spend a few days in the mountains. Almost on autopilot, he drives toward Matre and turns off toward Stordalen.

The first stretch after the turn follows a narrow road flanked by steep mountains. A wide river flows slowly through the valley, running alongside the road. Large boulders are scattered along the road and in the river, a testament to the natural forces that shaped the landscape. He continues and drives onto the construction road toward Stølsvatnet.

At the end of the road, where Maja's car was found, there's a small beach and a flat area perfect for camping. It's also an ideal starting point for mountain hikes, with several DNT trails beginning there.

After setting up camp, he builds a fire with the wood he brought, settles in with an ice-cold beer from the cooler, and gazes out over the water.

"What happened to you? Why did you choose to end your life right here?" he asks aloud. No one answers, and a few hours later, only embers remain of the fire.

The sun has long since set, and the temperature has dropped. He settles into his sleeping bag, the fresh mountain air quickly lulling him to sleep. In his dreams, he sees Maja, her sorrowful eyes calling out to him as she is slowly pulled into the depths. He wakes with a start, sits up, and for a moment doesn't know where he is. Still dazed, he steps out of the tent to relieve himself.

Outside, it's pitch dark, but when the moon peeks through the clouds, it sparkles like diamonds on the mountain lake. Mist and fog create a mystical atmosphere. Knut, who has never been tempted by what he calls superstitious nonsense, suddenly hears a sound he can't identify. It sounds like an animal, yet not quite —it's more like a whisper, almost as if someone is murmuring, something inhuman. The sound sends a chill down his spine.

The next morning, the sun shines in a clear sky, but

the dream and the strange experience from the night before still weigh on Knut's mind. It's unlike him to be so affected by his emotions. It must be this place, where a tragic suicide or accident most likely occurred, that's causing his imagination to play tricks on him.

After a good cup of coffee, sitting on a rock ledge by the water, he decides to follow the trail to Smalliegga, a small mountain that stands 886 meters above sea level. A short hike to clear his head is exactly what he needs. He packs some flatbread with ham spread, a banana, a chocolate bar, instant coffee, and a small gas burner in his bag.

The terrain is typical for western Norway—challenging, steep, and rugged. Fortunately, it's been dry and clear for a few days, so the ground is relatively dry. To reach the top, he follows the water for a while before the ascent begins. He stops to take in the view. Not a cloud in the sky, and everything is completely still.

Stepping off the trail for a short break, something glinting in the sun catches his attention—it looks like a piece of metal. Knut finishes up and walks toward the spot.

There, among some twigs, almost buried in moss, lies a tin can. The writing is nearly worn away by time, but he can just make out "Stavanger" and "sardines." The can is unopened, and the year 1938 is clearly stamped on the bottom. A bit puzzled by the find, he starts digging around.

"Maybe whoever lost the can dropped other things here as well?" he wonders.

He knows that war activities took place in these mountains, but finding something from that era feels significant. As he digs deeper through the branches and moss, he uncovers seven more cans—all the same brand and from the same year.

It occurs to him that this likely wasn't someone's forgotten packed lunch; it must be something more. He decides to take the cans to the Bjørn West Museum in Matre. Perhaps they can provide insight into the discovery.

Knut marks the spot with a long stick pushed firmly into the ground and continues his hike up to Smalliegga. At the summit, he unpacks his lunch, boils water for coffee, and makes himself comfortable. The view is spectacular. From here, he can see all the way to the Sognefjord in the west, and to the south, snow-covered peaks stretch as far as the eye can see. Autumn is coming to an end, and the first snow has already started to fall.

His thoughts turn to the soldiers who were stationed here during the war. It's hard to imagine how they managed. Little food, freezing winters, harsh landscapes, and the constant threat of being discovered by the Germans.

After a while, he packs up, puts on his backpack, and starts the descent back to the tent, with his car visible far below.

That evening, he lights another fire—it's simply part of the camping ritual. The desire to share these experiences with somcone is always present, but after his childhood sweetheart broke up with him years ago, no new woman has entered his life. The wounds from that breakup were too deep for him to risk getting hurt again. His parents often hint at the idea of finding a girlfriend; the comments about grandchildren are impossible to miss.

"Maybe one day," he thinks to himself.

As the embers of the fire die down, he crawls back into his sleeping bag. This night, the dreams stay away, and he sleeps soundly until the first rays of the sun hit the tent.

Solveig

2018

After the car with the two police officers drives away, Solveig stands there with tears in her eyes. It can't be true—she refuses to believe her mother is dead. For ten years, she has endured the accusations from her father, who still claims her mother tried to kill them all. Ten years of hatred and belittling. But now, it's enough; in just a few days, she will turn eighteen, and then he won't have control over her anymore. Her biggest wish is to get as far away from him as possible.

The gods know she's thought about running away many times, but leaving Laura and her two half-brothers, whom she loves more than anything, has stopped her every time. Kjersti needs her too. Her stepmother has become like a mother to her and Laura. Kjersti has always treated them as her own. The wicked stepmother from *Cinderella* has no place here—Kjersti is only kind and good. But she's powerless against Morten, who uses her as a punching bag whenever it suits him.

Her thoughts drift back to all the times Kjersti sacrificed herself when his bad temper was about to affect one of the boys. Each time, it was Solveig's job to calm and comfort her younger siblings.

In recent years, she has given up trying to persuade

Kjersti to leave him.

"I can't. He'll kill me," Kjersti whispered the last time they had to spend the night at the crisis center in Bergen. "No matter where we go, he'll come after us. The best way to protect you is to endure. And this time, he promised it won't happen again."

Solveig long ago stopped believing her father's false promises. They are just empty words he abandons whenever something doesn't go his way, or if someone forgets to tidy up toys, or anything else that ruins his perfect facade.

Most often, it's the eldest boy, Lars, who suffers. Even though he knows his father will get angry if he doesn't clean up, he still forgets. He's endured slaps, but the worst was when his father pulled down Lars's pants and beat him with a belt. Ten stinging lashes before Kjersti managed to get him to stop.

"The boy needs to learn how to behave. Coddling him like you do is useless," Morten had snarled at her. "But if you want to take the rest, go ahead. Maybe then he'll start behaving."

Morten dragged Kjersti into the bedroom, and judging by the sounds, she got her share too.

But he has never laid a hand on his daughters. She doesn't know why. And Laura, now thirteen, is her father's pride and joy. "Maybe it's because Mom disappeared? Does he feel guilty about something? Or does he pity us?" Solveig has often wondered but has never dared to ask. She's afraid of him—afraid of the violent outbursts that can come out of nowhere.

Thankfully, she has school and friends. When she's away from the house, she can disconnect completely, living like other teenagers—free as a bird and carefree. But the anxiety and pain are never far away, and as soon as she nears home, they return in full force.

"One day, I'll get far away from here," she says aloud to herself. That night, she dreams of the fire. She sees herself and Laura trapped in a sea of flames, screaming.

"Mom, Mom, where are you? It hurts! Help us," she cries.

Her mother's face appears, desperation in her eyes.

"Give me your hand, little one. Mom is here; everything will be alright," she whispers. "But hurry, the shadow is near; it's almost too late."

Desperately, Solveig stretches out her arm, trying to reach her. Just as their fingers barely touch, her mother is pulled back by strong forces. Fear gleams in her eyes, and a final, desperate cry escapes her lips.

"Solveig! Laura! My girls, I didn't mean it. Come back, don't leave me," she screams.

Solveig suddenly sits up in bed. The dream was so vivid it takes her several minutes to regain her composure. The idea that her mother wanted to kill her and Laura is something she can't comprehend.

There must be another explanation.

The next morning, Solveig finds the old photo album that belonged to Maja. Flipping through it always makes her feel closer to her mother. The first pages show pictures of her as a little girl. Smiling, she sits between a young couple, presumably her parents. All

Solveig knows is that they died in an accident when Maja was young, and her grandfather raised her after that.

On the next page, there are pictures of the house they lived in. One picture in particular stands out—a black-and-white photograph of an elderly couple holding hands on a wrought-iron bench outside the house.

Solveig remembers her mother telling her that the picture is of her grandparents, taken just weeks before her grandmother died. The way they look at each other shows that they must have loved each other deeply.

For a moment, Solveig wonders what happened to the old house. She can't remember ever being there. Her mother must have sold it after her grandfather passed away.

The next pages are harder to look at. The pictures of her as a newborn baby, cradled in Maja's arms, bring tears to her eyes. Then come several pages of photos of the two of them together.

"It must have been Dad who took the pictures," she thinks. "Mom looks happy. She's smiling at the camera."

On the next page, there's a picture from when Solveig was about three years old. She's naked, sitting in a pool by a mountain lake, smiling broadly while splashing in the water. She takes a closer look at the picture. The nature is stunning, like something out of a Norwegian travel ad. Was it just the two of them, or was her father there too? And where could this place be? She wishes she could ask her dad, but she knows that's impossible.

He doesn't like them talking about their mother; in fact, he has forbidden both Solveig and Laura from even mentioning her name.

Before turning the page, she takes the picture out of the plastic sleeve. As she flips it over, she's surprised to discover a note on the back: "Solveig and Maja. The secret place," followed by a heart and some numbers. Shaken by this unexpected discovery, Solveig wonders about the numbers. They aren't formatted like a date, and they don't look familiar. She's never seen anything like it before.

Curious, she types the numbers exactly as they are, with commas and spaces, into Google. A map quickly appears, revealing that the sequence of numbers is coordinates, and the secret place is in the Masfjord Mountains.

Determined to find out what might have happened to her mother, she slips the picture into her phone case. This is the first clue—actually, the only clue, aside from the car—that has surfaced since her mother disappeared. As soon as spring arrives and the weather improves, she plans to visit the place. After that, she will find her mother's childhood home, the place where Maja was once a happy little girl, unaware of how life would turn out.

It's too soon to share the discovery with Laura; her little sister doesn't remember much about life with Maja. Laura was only two years old when they returned from vacation to find the house burned down, with no trace of their mother. Time passed, and within a few weeks, Laura stopped asking about Mom. But Solveig never stopped longing for Maja. The longing had settled like a painful lump in her stomach. The lump is still there, but now something new has emerged: the excitement of discovery, a sense that she can finally do something.

She decides to keep this as her secret.

Ingvar

1982

The roar of the motorcycle lingered in the walls of the house long after Hans Arne and his partner, Sofie, sped away, the wind in their hair. Left behind on the porch, Ingvar stood holding a squirming Maja in his arms.

"I want to go too! I want to go too!" the little girl shouted.

"Not this time, little one. You're staying here with Grandpa. What should we do first? Maybe we should go say hello to the cow?" he said, smiling at her.

"Moo, moo!" said Maja, clapping her hands with delight. Her parents leaving and the fact that they had entrusted her to her grandfather, was already forgotten.

Taking care of the little one was a task Ingvar thoroughly enjoyed. After his beloved Kristine had passed away far too early, he had been lonely. The fact that his son had chosen to move into the old farmhouse with his girlfriend and daughter had completely changed his life. Not a single day went by without him spending time with his granddaughter, and the two had become close friends. But this weekend was the first time Maja would be staying overnight in the main house. Her parents had been invited to a wedding with friends in Stavanger and wouldn't return until Monday.

"We thought we'd take a little mini-vacation while

we're at it. Maybe drive to Oslo and back over the Hardangervidda. Test out a motorcycle trip and enjoy some time without the kid," Hans Arne had explained a few weeks earlier when he'd mentioned their plans to go away. "You'll do great as the babysitter," he added with a big smile.

After visiting the pasture gate and petting the cow, Ingvar and Maja walked back to the house. As soon as they were inside, Maja ran as fast as her little legs could carry her to the play corner in the living room. There, Ingvar had set out the old Lego bricks and toy cars that Hans Arne used to play with as a child. Ingvar went into the kitchen, put on some coffee, took out buns from the freezer, thawed them in the microwave, and set the table with butter, homemade blueberry jam, the buns, and a glass of milk for Maja.

Once the food was eaten, Maja hurried back to the Lego bricks. She was a calm child and could sit for long periods, babbling to herself while she worked intently on getting the bricks to stick together, only to tear them apart again afterward.

Ingvar sat down in the rocking chair by the window, letting his thoughts wander as he proudly watched his granddaughter. To think that Kristine never got to experience this. She would have loved being a grandmother. But fate had other plans.

Just five years earlier, she had discovered a lump in her breast. After a doctor's visit, followed by a mammogram and ultrasound, they had clung to the hope that the tumor would be benign. Unfortunately, it wasn't. Several months later, after many grueling radiation treatments and countless trips to the hospital, she had begged Ingvar to let her go.

"I can't take it anymore. My body has nothing left to give. I love you so much, but I can't fight this," she had almost whispered to him one evening as they lay at home in bed. "Don't take me to the hospital anymore. I want to be here, with you."

Heartbroken, Ingvar watched as she grew weaker and weaker. He fulfilled her final wish, caring for her at home until that beautiful spring day four years ago when she took her last breath and quietly passed away.

Hans Arne had taken time off from his business studies in the capital, and together with Sofie, he helped Ingvar with both the arrangements and the funeral. The rain had poured down as they carried the white coffin out of Sandnes Church. Tears streamed from both father and son, mixing with the heavy raindrops on the ground. Ingvar was standing alone by the gravesite after the coffin had been lowered into the earth, when the clouds suddenly parted, and a sunbeam struck him right in the heart.

"Goodbye, my beloved. Whether there's a heaven or not, I know that one beautiful day, we shall meet again," he whispered softly, casting one last red rose onto the coffin.

In the days and weeks after Kristine died, Ingvar had buried himself in work to keep occupied. Hans Arne had returned to Oslo and his studies, leaving the house unbearably empty. Every weekend, Ingvar went to the mountains, stocking up supplies at Didriksbu. In the mountains, he felt whole. Nature embraced him, letting him be himself, offering neither judgment nor pity when he sat quietly on a rocky ledge and let his tears flow freely. There, he found peace and reconciliation with himself.

Although the years were hard, Ingvar managed to get through them. So when Hans Arne brought Sofie home to celebrate Christmas nearly three years ago and they smiled, announcing they were expecting a child, he was overjoyed. His joy grew even greater when they asked if they could move into the old farmhouse—they wanted their child to grow up in the countryside.

As a newly graduated economist, Hans Arne quickly received a job offer from the Masfjorden municipality. Sofie, who had studied marine biology, was accepted into a temporary internship at the Institute of Marine Research in Matre. Things were looking bright for the young couple, who had no plans to marry.

"No one gets married these days; it's totally out of style," Hans Arne said when Ingvar wondered if it wouldn't be a good idea to formalize their relationship.

Ingvar saw no reason to push the issue. He was determined to let the young couple live exactly as they wished. He had no intention of becoming a grumpy old man but instead wanted to support and help them as much as possible. In fact, he thought they should have taken over the main house. According to tradition, it was his turn to move into the farmhouse. But Sofie wouldn't hear of it. She had fallen in love with the old house, and shortly after moving in, she was busy making it her own. The old timber walls were covered with plasterboard, then decorated with colorful wallpaper. Modern parquet floors were installed, and the electrical system was replaced. It turned out beautifully, and Ingvar had to admit that his daughter-in-law had good taste.

He would never forget the day they brought Maja home. When Sofie gently placed her in his arms, she opened her eyes and looked at him curiously. Ingvar's heart melted instantly.

"I'm afraid your father is going to spoil her rotten," Sofie said to Hans Arne one morning as they sat at the kitchen table, enjoying a cup of coffee. Ingvar had just stopped by and offered to push the little one around the yard in her stroller.

"But you know what? That's perfectly fine. It's wonderful to see how he lights up every time he sees her," she added with a smile.

"I agree, they're going to bring each other a lot of joy, and we're going to get a lot of babysitting," he replied, winking at her.

In the morning, Maja wakes up early.

"Get up, get up! Morning is here, Grandpa," she shouts, shaking Ingvar.

She doesn't give him a choice, and together they head down to the kitchen. After breakfast, they get dressed and go out to the barn. The farm isn't large, and they don't have many animals, just one cow and five hens impatiently waiting to be fed. Maja grabs the little basket and starts searching for eggs. With her tiny fingers, she finds three eggs hidden in the hay. Proudly, she shows them to Ingvar.

"Well, look at that, how clever you are. That means we'll have waffles for lunch," he says, patting her lightly on the head.

They spend the rest of the day on various chores around the farm. A flower bed needs weeding, the hedge needs trimming, and the gravel needs raking. Ingvar finds the small, simple tasks that Maja can help with. With great seriousness, she pulls up dandelions, puts them in her little wheelbarrow, and hauls them away.

"You've become quite the little farm girl. You're really good at this," he smiles at her.

In the evening, they sit on the sofa and watch children's TV. It's an episode of the classic *Madicken* by Astrid Lindgren, the one where Madicken climbs up on the roof, falls down, and gets a concussion.

"You have to promise me that you'll never do anything like that; it's dangerous," he says very seriously, looking at Maja. But Maja is already nodding off, and not long after, she falls asleep in his lap.

"It's been a long day, little one. I guess I'll just have to carry you to bed."

The next morning is Sunday, and it starts in exactly the same way. An early breakfast before they go out to feed the animals. Today, Maja finds five eggs. Proud as a little rooster, she's allowed to carry them all the way into the kitchen.

"Hm, waffles yesterday. What shall we make today? Maybe we'll just make an omelette for lunch?" Ingvar says to himself.

They spend this day outside as well. First, they go up to the hayloft, where Ingvar finds the old tricycle that used to belong to Hans Arne. Then he gets out the tools, and with Maja's help, they clean and oil the little vehicle. Afterward, it shines like new, and he lifts Maja onto the seat. Her feet don't quite reach the pedals, but Ingvar pushes her around the yard.

"In about a year, it'll fit you better," he says.

After Maja has been carried to bed, Ingvar settles into his favorite armchair with a book. He hasn't read more than a couple of pages when he hears a car outside. Shortly after, the doorbell rings.

"Who on earth could be out and about on a Sunday evening?" he wonders aloud before opening the door.

Outside stand the sheriff and the pastor, their faces serious. For a split second, the thought crosses his mind that they've come to tell him something has happened in the village, that they need his help.

But as quickly as that thought arises, he realizes that isn't the case. A visit from both the sheriff and the pastor at the same time can only mean one thing: someone has passed away.

"May we come in?" the sheriff asks. They've known each other for many years.

Ingvar opens the door fully and lets them into the

living room. His pulse has shot up to unknown heights, and he struggles to stay calm.

"I think you should sit down. Unfortunately, we have some bad news to share," the sheriff continues. "We just received a call from the police in Haukeli. There's been a serious accident. A car collided with a motor-cycle."

The blood drains from Ingvar's face, and he sinks heavily onto the sofa.

"There were two people on the motorcycle. A man and a woman. There's no easy way to say this, but both died instantly. It was a severe collision," the sheriff explains. "The couple hasn't been identified, but we have reason to believe it was your son and his girlfriend on the motorcycle."

Reason to believe. Not identified. Deceased. For a moment, Ingvar clings to the hope that there's been a mistake. It couldn't possibly be Hans Arne and Sofie.

No, this can't be true; they're supposed to come home tomorrow morning. But deep down, he knows it's true. He can feel it. His son too. Gone. How much more is he supposed to endure?

"Maja. She's upstairs, sleeping. The poor girl. How am I going to tell her this?" Ingvar breaks down in tears, sobbing with his face in his hands.

The pastor and the sheriff stay for several hours. There's no one else to call; Ingvar has no surviving relatives. Nor does Sofie have any close connections he can reach out to.

"My God, how am I going to take care of Maja alone?

This is too much; I can't handle this," he says, disbelief in his voice.

"We can contact child welfare for you; they can probably find a good foster home," the pastor says. "I'll ask them to come by and talk with you tomorrow."

Ingvar can only nod.

After the pastor and sheriff have driven away, he goes upstairs to check on the little one. He sits by her bedside and gently strokes her cheek.

The next morning, Ingvar is in a trance. The shocking news from the night before has kept him awake all night. Maja is her usual self—energetic and in a good mood.

"It's good that you're so little. Not once this weekend have you asked about Mommy and Daddy. But it's only a matter of time," Ingvar thinks to himself.

The doorbell rings. Outside stands a woman in her thirties.

"Hi, my name is Marit, and I'm from Child Welfare. The pastor called me and told me what had happened. May I come in?" she asks.

Ingvar lets her into the kitchen, where Maja is busy eating cereal.

"What a sweet little girl. What's your name?" Marit asks, ruffling Maja's hair.

"My name is A-ja," Maja says in her sweet little voice.

They go into the living room, where they can talk undisturbed. Marit explains that she has an emergency foster home ready and that she can take Maja with her when she leaves.

"I understand this must be difficult. It's not easy to care for a small child while you're in the midst of such terrible grief," she says sympathetically. "If you could pack some clothes for her, and maybe a teddy bear or something, we'll be on our way."

Still in shock, Ingvar packs Maja's bag and places her little blue stuffed bear, the one she sleeps with every night, on top where she can easily reach it. He hands the bag to Marit, who goes back to the kitchen to get Maja.

"Now you're going to come with me for a little while, dear. Grandpa needs some peace and quiet, you understand," she explains.

Maja looks at her skeptically but allows herself to be led into the hallway, where she puts on her shoes and jacket. Outside on the steps, she starts to realize that Grandpa isn't coming with her.

"Grandpa, Grandpa," she cries. "No, I want Grandpa, don't want to ride in the car, no, no."

From the kitchen, Ingvar can hear her screaming, and his heart breaks. What is he doing? What is happening? He bursts through the door, runs toward the screams, and takes a distraught Maja out of Marit's arms.

"This isn't going to work. You can't take her. She's all I have left, and I'm all she has," he shouts at Marit. "We'll manage, do you hear me? We'll make it."

Marit sighs heavily.

"Alright, fine. But I have to report this. We'll come

back in a few days to see how things are going," she says, getting into her car and driving back to the office in Knarvik.

Maja clings to him, and they sit down on the green-painted bench that has adorned the front of the house since Ingvar and Kristine moved in.

"I'm sorry, little one, I don't know what came over me. Imagine, I almost sent you away," he says, wiping a tear from Maja's cheek.

Finally, she calms down and looks at him. "Mean lady," she says with a serious tone. Ingvar can't help but smile and nods in agreement.

In the weeks that follow, Marit visits several times. The strong bond between Maja and Ingvar becomes more and more apparent, and after careful consideration, she decides to recommend that Ingvar be granted custody of the little one.

"It's always best for children to stay with family whenever possible. And most importantly, to grow up in familiar surroundings," she says to Ingvar one day as they sit on the small terrace outside the kitchen, drinking coffee. Maja is busy playing with her Lego blocks.

"You know, I lost my parents when I was quite young. My grandparents took care of me. Back then, I didn't think much about it, but it must have been very hard for them to cope with their own grief while also being strong for me. Now I understand what they went through," he replies, gazing out over the freshly mown fields. "Life never turns out the way you imagine it.

Sometimes I wonder what the meaning of it all is."

A few weeks later, when the postman delivers the official letter stating that he is now Maja's legal guardian, Ingvar sits down heavily on a stone by the mailbox. Maja hops and skips beside him, completely unaware of the new direction her life has taken.

As small as she is, she has only asked about Mommy and Daddy a few times, but Ingvar knows that in a year or two, all her memories of her parents will be gone.

His own memories can never be erased; the grief and pain will stay with him for the rest of his life. But for Maja's sake, he promises himself, right then and there, that he will do everything he can to give her a good and carefree life.

Maja

2019

By the end of March, everything in the mountain region has returned to normal. After a bitterly cold winter with little precipitation, the snowmelt came early, followed by weeks of sleet and rain. The mountain lakes once again reach acceptable levels, covering the craters that had been visible since last fall. All the construction workers packed up, and the equipment and temporary barracks were transported away, precariously balanced on large semi-trailers that barely managed the tight turns down to Matre. Peace and order have been restored.

For Maja, spring marks the beginning of a new season of preparation for gathering and harvesting. All the jam she made last season has been consumed. She cleans the jars, getting them ready for a new round of delicious blueberry, cloudberry, and lingonberry preserves. The pantry in the bunker is stocked with enough sugar to make jam for at least two years. It is still a bit early to pick berries—nothing will be ripe until later in the summer.

But it is the perfect time to start the fishing season. Her grandfather had taught her that fish bite best right after the ice melts and the temperatures in the mountain lakes begin to rise. That's when the fish start moving around more after a long winter of being mostly still. From experience, she knows the fish aren't as picky about what they eat at this time, making them much easier to catch.

One of her favorite lakes isn't far from Didriksbu. It is fairly large but not one of the most visited, so she can fish there for hours without being disturbed.

April brings some warm, pleasant spring days, so Maja packs her daypack and heads out for the first fishing trip of the season. The fishing rod she uses is one of Ingvar's old ones, and it works just as well now as it did fifty years ago. Besides, it is nostalgic, and it feels like her grandfather is there, watching over her.

When she reaches the lake, she prepares the rod with her favorite lure: a silver-colored, fish-shaped hook with touches of gold and red. A trick her grandfather taught her was to attach a fly a few centimeters from the hook.

"It's called trailing a fly. The trout thinks the hook is a competitor trying to steal its prey, so it'll go for the fly. And just like that, you've got it," he had explained seriously on one of the fishing trips they took when she was a little girl.

"The best is to use a double-hooked wet fly, but a streamer or a large nymph works too."

Her grandfather's words come to mind as clearly as the sun on a beautiful spring day.

Once the rod is prepared, according to all the rules of the art, it is time for the first cast. With experienced fingers, she releases the reel, holds a finger over the fishing line, stretches the rod behind her, then casts it forward, letting go of the line at just the right moment. The rod makes a soft swishing sound, and she enjoys watching the hook and fly sail through the air.

The cast isn't far, but it doesn't take long before she gets a bite. Maja slowly reels it in, and from the depths emerges the first trout. It is shiny and sleek, more than big enough for a couple of dinners.

Over the next few hours, she catches twelve more trout. Pleased with herself, she takes a break and pulls out her portable stove and frying pan. She guts one of the smaller fish and fries it. With nothing but a little salt, she enjoys the taste of freshly caught trout, cooked right where it was caught.

As the day draws to a close, she keeps fishing until she has twenty glistening trout lined up in the heather. Quickly, she guts them, puts them in a bag, and packs them in her backpack.

Back at the cabin, a meowing Doffen awaits. He had smelled the fish from a distance and knew what was coming. Impatient as a small child, he winds around Maja's legs, meowing loudly.

"Relax, you little rascal, you'll get some soon," she laughs, patting him on the head.

She then takes one of the fish heads and places it on the stone slab outside the entrance. Doffen takes his time sniffing and licking the treat before crunching through the skin, eyes, and bones.

"I bet that was good, huh? Nothing beats fresh fish,

we can agree on that," she says, watching the cat enjoy his meal.

Near the cabin entrance, Maja had set up a small drying shed made of stone. She hangs all the fish heads there, while bringing the rest of the fish inside. To preserve the fish for the winter, she had experimented with various methods. Salting and drying were ancient preservation techniques that Maja had become quite comfortable with in recent years. But marinating had also become a favorite. Last fall, she had collected various plants and herbs she found in the wild. Everything had been hanging to dry inside the cabin, and now she has a whole supply of herbs and spices to use in trout marinade, along with wild garlic, which she had picked fresh in the lowlands a few days ago. It is best in the spring when the long, grass-like blades aren't as fibrous as they would be later in the season.

Maja layers all the fish with coarse salt in a bucket and places it in the cold bunker. Afterwards, she sits down with a cup of tea, made from rose hips she had picked last year, and smiles contentedly.

Her interest in edible wild plants came from Ingvar, who had taught her about the most common varieties like dandelion, wild garlic, rose hips, and nettles. After she moved in with Morten and became a homemaker, she had nurtured this foraging hobby as often as she could.

The house they had lived in was at the end of a forest road. Nature was right outside the window, and Maja often went for walks to gather mushrooms and berries.

After reading up on the subject in several books borrowed from the library, she experimented with nettle soup and various dried herbs in her bread baking.

Morten didn't care about her hobby, so she kept it to herself. She refrained from mentioning that she sometimes added wild-harvested ingredients to their meals. However, he did appreciate homemade blueberry jam, so she always made sure they had plenty. She could spend hours in the woods picking berries every fall. What she didn't have time to turn into jam, she stored in the freezer to make more during the winter months.

After the humiliating doctor's appointment, where both the doctor and Morten claimed she was a psychopath, she was prescribed antidepressants. For a while, she took the pills every day, but she noticed they made her sluggish. So, she stopped taking them without telling Morten. Instead, she flushed a pill down the toilet every day so he wouldn't discover what she was doing. Everything went fine for a long time.

To anyone encountering them on one of their Sunday walks in the woods behind their house, they would have appeared to be an ordinary family. But beneath the surface, Morten's mood was always a lurking threat. A dark shadow would come over him from time to time, and when that happened, everything she did or said was wrong. Maja tried to shield the girls as best she could, but it wasn't easy. They always burst into tears whenever Morten slammed his hand on the table because the potatoes were slightly undercooked, or the sauce had developed a skin. The repeated episodes made Maja jumpy. In front of the girls, she tried to appear calm and composed, even though it took a great deal of self-control.

When Laura turned one, they celebrated with ice cream and cake. The girls had a wonderful time, and Solveig gave her little sister a gift she had made herself—a drawing of the two of them in their beds in the room they shared. Laura pointed to the drawing and exclaimed, "Sol." Delighted that her first word was Solveig's nickname, they tried, unsuccessfully, to get her to say "Mommy" and "Daddy" as well. In the evening, after the children had fallen asleep, they sat on the sofa with a glass of wine each.

"Now it's almost perfect. All we're missing is a boy, someone to carry on my name. You know how much that means to me," Morten said. "You need to stop taking the pill. This time, it's going to be right—I can feel it."

Maja had dreaded this conversation for a whole year, but now she gathered her courage.

"Morten, I can't have any more children," she said quietly. "The doctor told me after the surgery when Laura was born. He couldn't be certain, but he didn't seem optimistic. There were complications. I haven't been taking the pill, hoping he was wrong, but I haven't gotten pregnant." Morten went completely silent. Without warning, he took his wine glass and hurled it violently at the wall behind the TV.

"And you're just now telling me this? Damn it, Maja,

I didn't expect this from you. But I guess it's not surprising from someone as mentally unstable as you. You're useless, and now you've really proven it," he said calmly before getting up and going to the bedroom.

Maja followed him, pleading for his forgiveness.

"I'm so sorry. I knew how disappointed you'd be. I couldn't bring myself to tell you," she said in a trembling voice.

The next moment, she felt a stinging pain as Morten's fist struck her cheek. She collapsed onto the bed, and Morten pounced on her.

"You're not worthy. Far beneath my station. I should never have married you," he screamed as he tightened his hands around her throat. "You deceitful bitch, lured me in with those innocent eyes, and it turns out you're the devil himself."

Maja fought for her life. The air in her lungs was running out when he suddenly let go. She gasped loudly. Then she felt him start to tear at her clothes and pull off her pants. It was futile to resist; he was far too strong. After he was finished, she lay bruised and helpless on the bed.

"That's what happens to lying whores," he said heartlessly as he pulled a bag from the closet and began stuffing it with clothes. "I can't stand to be here any longer. From now on, you're on your own."

Shattered, both by guilt for deceiving him and by physical pain, Maja managed to get up the next morning. The face that looked back at her in the mirror was covered in bruises and swelling. She carefully tried to cover the worst of it with makeup. Solveig watched her curiously but said nothing. It was as if she understood that her mother was in pain. All day, she was extra attentive and took care of her little sister so Maja could rest on the sofa. When their father didn't come home for dinner as usual, neither of the girls asked about him. But when several days passed without him showing up, Maja became convinced that he had left them for good.

It was only after a week that he returned. He brought his friend Per, and they were driving a van. Without so much as looking at her or the girls, they carried out the sofa and the TV. Then he went to the bedroom and retrieved more clothes, along with some boxes of papers and books.

"I'll come back for the girls later," he said confidently before walking over to them and lifting Solveig. "Daddy is arranging a new home where we'll live without your psychopathic mother. Everything will be fine."

He kissed her on the cheek before putting her down and leaving in the van with Per.

Helpless, Maja stood on the porch with Laura in her arms and Solveig close by. She hadn't prepared for this. Panic threatened to overwhelm her. Without the girls, she was nothing. Back in the kitchen, she took out her cell phone and Googled "lawyer." Soon several names appeared, but a woman advertising family law caught her attention. Maja dialed the number and reached attorney Trude Mjanger.

After hearing Maja explain the situation, Trude said

she had a cancellation and could meet with Maja in an hour or two if she could come by. Her office was in downtown Bergen, so Maja took the girls and caught the bus.

Trude Mjanger was a full-figured woman in her forties, dressed in a pantsuit that accentuated her rounded curves. Her hair and makeup were flawless, and Maja liked her immediately.

"You know what? I'll have my assistant take the children to the break room and give them some snacks so we can talk without interruptions," Trude said.

Soon after, a young woman entered the office, scooped Laura into her arms, and took Solveig by the hand. The girls were trusting, but Solveig glanced at Maja, seeking reassurance. Maja nodded, and they left the room.

"You mentioned that you've been a stay-at-home mom and the primary caregiver for the girls. That gives you a strong case for primary custody," Trude said confidently. "Don't worry—we'll take care of every-thing. I'll draft a letter to send to him tomorrow, making it clear that if he tries to take the children, he'll be reported to the police for kidnapping. That usually stops men like him," she added with a wink.

"What's his new address? You don't know? Don't worry, I'll find out—trust me."

A few hours later, Maja and the girls were back at the house at the end of the road. Overwhelmed by the day's events, the children quickly fell asleep after Maja tucked them in.

Maja sat down at the kitchen table, trying to organize her thoughts. What would become of her now? How would she support herself? Life with Morten hadn't been perfect, but now she was completely alone. All she had ever wanted was for them to be a happy family.

She sighs heavily. The memories of the weeks after Morten had left are still painful. She takes out her diary and begins writing down her thoughts. Afterward, she returns it to its usual place on the bookshelf above the wood stove. Writing has become her therapy; the words she puts on paper take on a life of their own, helping to clear her mind. But each session leaves her emotionally drained—it is exhausting to relive those painful memories.

As the day comes to a close, Maja puts away the fishing gear. Pleased with her efforts, she crawls into bed and quickly falls asleep.

Outside, the moon has just risen, casting its light over the rocky slope, down to the stream, and illuminating the small pond at the bottom of the valley. Doffen stretches out on the stone slab by the front door, shakes his head a little, and prepares for another night of exciting mouse hunting.

Solveig

2019

In the mailbox, there's a letter addressed to Solveig. The sender is the Nordhordland District Court. With trembling hands, she opens the envelope and pulls out the document, revealing the court's decision regarding her mother.

She quickly reads the brief note, then folds it and puts it back in the envelope. Rushing home, she goes straight to her room and sits heavily on her bed, her mind in chaos. Mom is dead. The court has confirmed it. No one will search for her; the case is closed.

Tomorrow, after school, she will seek out the police officer with the kind eyes—maybe he can help her figure out what might have happened.

The hours drag by. The teacher drones on about fauna in Science class, but Solveig can't concentrate. Normally, she'd be engaged—science is one of her favorite subjects—but today, her thoughts are elsewhere. Finally, the school day ends. She quickly packs her things, and, the first to leave, nearly runs out of the classroom, heading straight for the Knarvik Center.

The police station is on the third floor of one of the largest buildings. Behind the counter sits a stern-looking woman with thick-rimmed glasses.

She barely glances at Solveig.

"What do you want?" she asks sourly, returning her attention to the solitaire game on her computer.

"I was wondering if I could speak to the police officer who was at our house a few weeks ago?" Solveig asks cautiously.

"And what's his name?" the woman asks gruffly.

"I'm not sure, but it's about my mother. She's been declared dead," Solveig replies.

Just as the woman is about to brush her off, Knut appears in the doorway.

"Can you check something for me?" he asks the receptionist.

"Of course, no problem. What do you need?" she responds in a sickeningly sweet tone, instantly forgetting about Solveig.

Knut glances at the girl by the counter.

"Hi, I've seen you before. Your name is Solveig, right?" he asks with a smile. He gestures for her to follow him past the receptionist, who shoots her a sour look, and into his office.

"Sorry about the mess. Paperwork keeps piling up, and I can't seem to stay on top of it," he apologizes. "Would you like something to drink? Coffee, soda?"

"No, thanks. I'm fine," Solveig says, sitting in the chair he clears for her by moving a jacket and some books.

"How are you doing?" Knut asks sympathetically. His kind eyes and gentle voice are too much for Solveig, and she begins to cry. The tears come in torrents, as if a dam has burst, and she can't stop. The grief and pain she's suppressed since learning of her mother's disappearance flood out.

Knut hands her a tissue.

"All my life, I've been waiting for Mom to come back," she says through sobs. "I never believed she could be dead. Dad always blamed her for trying to kill us, but I don't believe that. I was only eight, but I remember her. The last thing she told me was to take good care of my little sister, Laura, and not to worry about her."

Solveig looks at Knut with tear-filled eyes.

"But why did she leave? Why didn't she take us with her? Could she have planned her own death to escape him?" she asks desperately.

"I don't know if we'll ever get all the answers you need," Knut replies gently. "People's actions can be hard to understand, but I'm sure your mother loved you very much. You might not remember, but I was at your house about ten years ago. We had some questions for her, and you were the one who answered the door."

"Was that you? Yes, I remember. It was both exciting and scary seeing the police at the door," Solveig says, managing a small smile.

"I remember your mother held you protectively. She seemed like the kind of person who would do anything to keep you safe," Knut says.

Solveig is reminded of a class trip to Voss a few years ago. They had rented a cabin for the weekend. Early one Saturday, she and some friends were playing soccer by the water when she noticed a woman sitting on a nearby bench. The woman was unkempt, wearing a dark cap that hid her face. Solveig thought she might be homeless, but there was something about the way the woman got up, slung a backpack over her shoulder, and walked away with determined steps that felt familiar. At the time, she couldn't place it, but now, sitting in Knut's office, it hits her. Could it have been her mother sitting on that bench? Did Maja know Solveig was in Voss that weekend?

"Could she be living under a new identity, maybe even homeless?" Solveig asks, her voice filled with desperation.

Knut looks at her, understanding how hard it is for her to accept the truth.

"It would be impressive if someone managed to stay hidden for ten years like that. Sooner or later, people ask questions," he says.

With a sigh, Solveig stands up. She hasn't gotten any closer to solving her suspicions that her mother is still alive, but at least Knut had listened without ridiculing her. She shakes his hand solemnly.

"Thank you for listening. I'll probably never stop hoping Mom is alive, even though everyone says she's dead."

"Letting go is one of the hardest things to do," Knut says kindly. "It was very nice talking to you. Feel free to come by anytime."

Solveig has to catch the bus home, but the conversation with Knut has lightened her spirits.

There's no one else she can talk to about Mom—Dad's eyes turn dark the moment she mentions her.

Solveig's friends know parts of her story, but this is too big to share with any of them. In a few days, she has to go to a lawyer's office in Bergen, and she intends to do it alone—no one needs to know.

The law firm is located down by Bryggen, one of the more exclusive areas. The entrance is adorned with neatly maintained pink and purple petunias. Inside, a board displays the firm's name in gold lettering. Solveig climbs the three flights of stairs, finds the door marked *Aksdal, Kvinge, and Kvinesdal*, and steps into a cozy waiting room where a smiling receptionist greets her. She's asked to take a seat and wait until they are ready.

A bit nervous, Solveig sits on the edge of a chair. On the coffee table, there are several magazines, one of which is from the Norwegian Tourist Association. A headline on the cover catches her attention: *From Cabin to Cabin in the Masfjord Mountains*. But it's the photo in the accompanying article that makes her gasp. The picture shows a mirror-like lake on a bright, sunny summer day. At the far end of the water, a small mountain pasture is visible. The caption reads, *Stølsvatnet in Stordalen*. It's the same lake where her mother's car was found.

Suddenly, she hears her name being called repeatedly. Solveig snaps out of her trance. A man is speaking to her. She stands and follows him into a meeting room where two people are seated at a large, polished mahogany table. The men introduce themselves as Aksdal, Kvinge, and Kvinesdal. She's directed to an empty chair at the end of the table.

Kåre Kvinge, a man in his sixties, begins to speak.

"Nice to finally meet you, Solveig. I remember your great-grandfather well—he was an exceptionally pleasant and sociable man," he says with a warm smile.

Solveig looks from one lawyer to the other, surprised. She wasn't expecting this. All three of them know her mother's family. But she knows almost nothing. Since her mother disappeared, there has been no one to ask.

"It's unfortunate that we meet under such circumstances. We had hoped, right up until the last moment, that Maja would reappear. But now that she's been declared dead, it's our duty to ensure that her inheritance goes to the right people," Kvinge continues. "Since you are of legal age, you will receive your share now. Your sister, however, must wait until she turns eighteen. Until then, we've been appointed by the state to manage her funds in her best interest."

Still in shock, Solveig tries to maintain a calm and composed demeanor, though inside she feels completely overwhelmed.

"Shall we dive right in?" Aksdal asks, looking at her. "Would you like something to drink? There's a lot to cover."

A bottle of Coke and a crystal glass are placed in front of her. She pours a little into the delicate glass and takes a small sip. The lawyer opens his folder, puts on his reading glasses, clears his throat, and begins to read.

Two hours later, he closes the folder and hands it to Solveig.

"I think we've covered everything. I understand this is a lot to process. You now have control over your share, but we'd be happy to continue assisting you. Take a few days to think it over, and let us know when you've made a decision."

The three lawyers shake her hand solemnly and wish her luck. Soon, she's back on the street, where life goes on as usual, with people hurrying past, indifferent to the fact that Solveig's world has just been turned upside down.

On the bus back to Knarvik, Solveig tries to process everything she's learned. Mom was raised by her grandfather after losing her parents at a young age. Solveig knew that, but she didn't know the details. There were no surviving close relatives—just the two of them. A wave of sadness washes over her. How little she knows about her mother's history. She blames her dad; he never wanted to talk about Mom. She decides not to confront him. This will be her secret. She won't even tell Laura—not until she's of legal age, too.

She thinks back to what else Kåre Kvinge had told her.

"Your great-grandfather, Ingvar, worked for the same company for many years. During that time, he acquired quite a few shares, both purchased and gifted. He also invested in other companies, many of which have grown significantly. When he passed away, your mother inherited everything, but she never touched the shares. Their value has increased considerably, and the total estate is estimated at about 50 million kroner. In addition, there's the property in Masfjorden, valued at eight million, largely due to the expansive land in Stølsheimen. And then there are the savings and checking accounts, which hold around two million kroner."

Before she left, they had given her the key to a safe deposit box, along with all the necessary documents.

"We've kept this safe for your mother. It was her wish that you inherit it. We don't know what's inside, but now you have the authority to open it. The box is located at Sparebanken Vest in Knarvik."

Dazed by all the information, Solveig thinks she might wait to open the safe deposit box until Laura can share the secret. Later that evening, she places the key in her mother's old jewelry box and hides it in a drawer in her dresser.

The following weekend, she borrows Kjersti's car, claiming she's meeting some classmates. The truth is something else entirely. She's finally going to visit Masfjordnes, the place where her mother and great-grandfather lived—the property she's now inherited.

As she drives into the yard of the small farm, she is struck by how idyllic it is. The sun is shining, the thermometer shows minus four degrees, and although the ground is frosty, there's no snow. The fjord gleams in the sunlight.

"How lucky you were to grow up in such a beautiful place, Mom," she whispers to herself.

By the entrance to the main house, a green-painted bench sits. Most of the paint has peeled away, and some of the wooden planks are rotting. An inscription plate is attached to the back of the bench, but the lettering has faded over time. She recognizes the bench from a photograph in an old album—a picture of her great-grandparents, Ingvar and Kristine.

Solveig takes out the key and unlocks the door. A stale smell greets her as she steps inside. Without paying much attention to it, she walks through the hall-way and into the living room. The red velvet corner sofa is faded and worn. The simple interior suggests that those who lived here didn't care much about design. Several pictures of Maja as a little girl hang on the walls. One, the largest, draws Solveig's attention. It shows a smiling Maja sitting on a motorcycle with a young couple. The picture was taken outside in the yard.

"If only you were all alive. I would have loved to know you." Emotions overwhelm her, and she has to sit down for a moment.

"You grew up without your mother, too. It seems we have something in common." Tears well up.

Once she collects herself, she continues exploring the house. The kitchen feels like a time capsule. A small lace cloth and an artificial potted plant sit on the Formica table under the window.

Empty pots line the windowsill—it's been a long time

since any live plants filled them. Solveig opens the cupboard above the steel sink. Mugs from Sparebanken Vest, various sports teams, and one from the old Sandnes bakery greet her. Several cups are missing handles. On the shelf above, there's an older dinner set from the Porsgrund porcelain factory.

She closes the cupboard and heads upstairs. The bedroom on the left has a neatly made bed with a large crocheted blanket on top. Several stuffed animals of varying ages and conditions are arranged on it. Solveig sits on the bed, realizing this must have been her mother's room. A small desk in one corner is covered in a thin layer of dust. A stack of notebooks lies neatly piled. She picks up the one on top. In cursive hand-writing, it reads: *Belongs to Maja Sandnes, 1st grade, Sandnes School.*

Solveig returns to the kitchen. A bulletin board next to the fridge holds several keys. She selects the one for the old caretaker's house.

This house also shows signs of long neglect. Lawyer Kvinge had mentioned it was rented out occasionally, but it's been a while since the last tenants left. Despite the disuse, the house has a certain charm. The walls are mostly covered in vibrant, patterned wallpaper from the 1980s, but the original log-house style is preserved in the living room ceiling and the upstairs bedrooms.

Though she doesn't find anything of personal value from either Maja or Ingvar, Solveig still feels a strong presence of both. Standing on the front steps, she looks around. On the upper side of the main house is a large barn. She decides to explore it next time.

She gets into the car and turns the ignition. She hadn't noticed the cold while walking through the houses and around the property, but now her body is trembling, and she cranks the heater to full blast. The overwhelming impressions leave her staring straight ahead for nearly an hour. This place is hers now. She will live here. When spring comes and her exams are over, she will make a decision. The time has come to cut ties with her father. He's caused enough damage.

Maybe she can convince Kjersti to move here with their younger siblings. They can all leave him behind. The thought appeals to her. Yes, that's the solution— they'll move here, and their father can be left alone in the empty house, regretting everything he's done.

Maja

2020

"New year, new opportunities." Maja reflects on the old saying her grandfather would repeat every New Year's Eve. Sitting alone in the mountains, with only a cat for company, those words no longer hold any meaning for her.

Outside, a bitter January wind seeps through every crack, and the cold has reached her heart. No matter how much she stokes the fire, she can't get warm. She knows why all too well—this isn't the first time she's felt a cold that penetrates to the bone. This year marks twenty years since he died. Dear, sweet Grandpa.

He had suffered from severe stomach pain for months before Maja finally convinced him to see a doctor. After several examinations at Haraldsplass Diaconal Hospital, the diagnosis was grim: colon cancer with metastasis.

"Unfortunately, there's not much we can do, other than keep you comfortable," the doctor said gently. "If there are things you need to take care of, I'd do them now. You don't have much time."

Ingvar took the news calmly. Finally, he would have peace. Finally, he would reunite with those he had lost. Though never religious, as death approached, he couldn't help thinking of his parents, Didrik, Kristine, and especially his son—waiting for him somewhere in the universe. But the thought of leaving Maja alone overshadowed the calm that had settled over him.

"I've lived a long, good life, but with many sorrows. Death doesn't scare me; I welcome it," he reassured the doctor.

The next day, he contacted the young lawyer, Kåre Kvinge, the son of a childhood friend, and entrusted all the practical matters to him.

Maja was devastated. She dropped out of Knarvik High School to stay home in Masfjordnes to care for him. Ingvar was grateful for her company, though he wished she took her studies more seriously.

"You need a good education, my dear Maja," he often repeated. "Sitting here with an old man won't get you anywhere."

No matter how many times he urged her to return to school, Maja refused to leave his side. As the end neared, and he needed help around the clock, she remained steadfast.

"I'll never leave you," she insisted. "You'd do the same for me if the roles were reversed."

That New Year's Eve, Maja made pinnekjøtt, as usual. The scent filled the house. She set the table in the kitchen with the freshly ironed lace tablecloth her grandmother had embroidered and the finest china. When the food was ready, she helped Ingvar to the table. He was having a good day and managed to sit with her for a little while. Neither of them ate much, but the sense of normalcy, of pretending everything was okay, made the meal special.

Later, she helped Ingvar back to bed. When the clock struck midnight, he was still awake. In a hoarse voice, he managed to say his usual phrase:

"New year, new opportunities. Never forget that, my dear Maja."

The next morning, the nurse came by to give him morphine.

"It's not long now. Would you like to sit with him?" she asked gently.

Terrified, Maja quickly dressed and took her place by his bedside. She held his hand, stroking his cheek. For a brief moment, he opened his eyes and looked at her.

"Kristine," he whispered, before closing his eyes for the last time. He took a few final, rasping breaths, and then everything went silent.

"Goodbye, Grandpa. I love you," Maja whispered, kissing him on the forehead. Then she collapsed into uncontrollable, overwhelming sobs until the nurse helped her back to her feet.

"Is there anyone I can call?" the nurse asked. "You shouldn't be alone right now."

"There's no one. I don't need anyone. It's just me now," Maja replied. For the first time in her eighteen years, she was truly alone. No relatives, no close friends.

After the funeral home took Ingvar's body, neighbors came by to pay their respects. Maja didn't feel like talking but let them in and let them take over. One neighbor, in particular, took charge—it was the mother of Kåre Kvinge, the lawyer who later went over the financial matters with Maja.

"Everything is under control. You don't need to worry about anything. Ingvar left everything to you, and the paperwork is ready," Kvinge explained.

After the funeral, when the house had emptied of neighbors and friends, Maja sank onto the sofa and stayed there for three days. On the morning of the fourth day, her grandfather's last words came back to her: "New year, new opportunities."

"Life must go on," she thought. "But not here. There are too many memories."

She spent the rest of the day closing up the house. She washed the dishes, made the beds, packed a suitcase with clothes, and took the large photo album. Then she remembered something her grandfather had told her years ago. It was one evening after they'd watched a TV program about people in America building hideouts in the woods in case of nuclear war. Maja had found the idea amusing, but Ingvar had turned serious.

"Maja, there's something you need to know. In my closet, at the very bottom, there's a gray backpack. If something happens to me, or if there's a war, you must promise me to take that backpack. It contains everything you'll need," he had said.

She went to his bedroom one last time. The sight of the empty bed tore at her heart. In the closet, she moved aside boxes of papers and old shoes until she found the gray backpack. Without checking the contents, she slung it over her shoulder.

After locking up the barn and the two houses, she stood at the bus stop and took the bus to Bergen.

A friend from secondary school let Maja sleep on her couch in her small apartment until she could find her own place. It didn't take long before Maja landed a job as a waitress in one of the city's many restaurants, and a new life began. She worked almost every evening, which suited her well. She could sleep late, get up, and go straight to work—no time to think, no time to mourn.

In the restaurant, Maja felt like an actress. The tables, chairs, and guests were her stage extras, and she performed the same play every night. Smiling, balancing trays, serving plates of steaming food, and obeying every order from the maître d', she played her role perfectly.

Life in Bergen went on. This new existence consumed her, and she gave herself no time to pause—until the one-year anniversary. She had worked late on New Year's Eve, but the next day, her day off, reality hit hard. It had been a whole year since her grandfather died. The pain struck her like a punch in the gut, and she gasped, collapsing onto the kitchen floor. For an entire year, she had suppressed her grief, refusing to feel anything. But now, all the memories came flooding back, leaving her dizzy.

"How could you leave me, Grandpa?" she sobbed. "What will become of me?"

A few hours later, Maja retrieved the backpack she

had hidden at the top of her closet and sat down on the sofa. It was time to see what it contained. What secrets had her grandfather kept from her?

The cord was tightly knotted, and it took her some time to open it. The first thing she found was a map with a large area circled in red marker and a small cross in the middle. "Didriksbu," she read. She spread the map out on the coffee table and saw it depicted the Stølsheimen mountain area.

Maja emptied the backpack's contents onto the table: a compass, a pocketknife, first aid supplies, a small cooking pot and gas burner, matches, a wind sack, an emergency blanket, fishing gear, coffee, some instant soup packets, dry biscuits, and an envelope labeled "Maja." Puzzled, she opened the letter, written in her grandfather's neat handwriting.

Dear Maja,

if you are reading this letter, I am no longer here. Now it's your turn to carry this legacy forward. Didriksbu contains everything you need to survive for many years. It's a refuge I hope you will never need. Don't tell anyone about this. Not even a future husband. This must remain top secret—promise me that. The area is part of the property in Masfjorden, and no one knows about it.

Love you always.
Take care of yourself, and be happy.

The letter was signed Grandpa Ingvar.

Stunned, Maja put the letter down and glanced over the table. That her grandfather had never mentioned this secret place, far up in the mountains, shocked her. It seemed too incredible to be true. She packed everything back into the backpack.

"When summer comes, I'll take this map and find Didriksbu," she thought, her curiosity piqued and a small spark of excitement spreading through her body.

"You were full of secrets, weren't you, Grandpa? I never would've guessed," she said aloud, as if he were sitting beside her.

After this discovery, life became a little easier for Maja. She started taking long hikes in the city mountains during her free time and occasionally went out with friends.

But just a few weeks before her planned expedition to Didriksbu, she ran into Morten again, and her life took a new turn. All her plans were put on hold, and the backpack remained untouched in the closet.

It wasn't until several years later—on that fateful night when she killed her children—that she retrieved the backpack again. Even in the midst of chaos, she had managed to put on her green mountain pants, Gore-Tex jacket, and sturdy hiking boots. She packed an extra set of wool underwear into the backpack.

On her way, she stopped at an ATM and withdrew ten thousand kroner. Then she followed the E39 toward Matre, where she turned off toward Stordalen. According to the map, the easiest way to reach

Didriksbu was from Stølsvatnet, a place she had visited with her grandfather several times. But why he had never taken her further up into the mountains to show her Didriksbu remained a mystery.

Upon arriving at Stølsvatnet, Maja threw her mobile phone as far as she could into the water. Then she rolled down the driver's side window, got out, leaned in, and carefully released the handbrake. The car immediately rolled down the steep slope into the water. It didn't take long before the rear end quietly disappeared into the depths. Maja hung the map case around her neck, slung the backpack over her shoulders, and set off toward an uncertain fate.

Once again, Maja finds herself lost in memories. Everything had been scribbled in the diary, now nearly full. Writing has helped, even though it is painful. Organizing her thoughts brings her some peace. She believes Ingvar must have felt the same way during the times he stayed at Didriksbu alone.

The discovery of the notes Ingvar had hidden deep in a cabinet in the bunker had answered many of her questions. In a carefully updated logbook, he had described the construction of Didriksbu in simple terms. Reading between the lines, she sensed the pain he must have carried, from hiding there as a boy in a pile of planks to years later, when he lay there feverish after his grandparents had died.

The last entry in the notebook was from the autumn before Ingvar passed away. It read:

"Annual inspection completed. Everything okay. Some expired canned goods. Small leak above the entrance repaired."

The first time Maja came to Didriksbu, she didn't care about anything. A roof over her head, simple food like canned goods and dry biscuits, and a wood stove to heat the cabin during the cold winter months had allowed her to survive that first year. Most of her time was spent lying in bed, staring blankly ahead.

Apathy and suppression, mixed with grief and nightly nightmares, were all she needed. It wasn't until a year later, after she returned with Doffen following her failed suicide attempt, that she began to take an interest in the cabin.

With fresh eyes, Maja reentered Didriksbu, slowly but surely taking ownership of the structure her grandfather had left her. She worked diligently, first retrieving her grandfather's notes from the bunker. In the same cabinet, she found several other useful items, including books on fishing, trapping, and a thick guide on foraging.

But the most remarkable discovery was a book about the Bjørn West forces. It told the story of how a guerrilla force had formed in Stølsheimen during World War II, with the names and photos of young men who had escaped the Germans' sinister plans to send them to the Russian front.

The shock was immense when she recognized her grandfather's name beneath a photo of a handsome young man in a Home Guard uniform. The caption revealed that he had been wounded by German bullets but had managed to hide in the mountains for a week before being found. Next to Ingvar's picture was another of a man named Didrik, described as having been shot and killed by the Germans.

"My God, Grandpa, were you part of the resistance? Shot?" Maja whispered to herself. "I think I'm starting to understand. You must have hidden here. Didrik was your friend, wasn't he? Is that why you named the cabin after him?"

Tears streamed down her cheeks.

"Poor Grandpa, all you went through, and you never told me a thing," she sobbed.

These new discoveries shifted her perspective on life. Didriksbu now carried a new significance. In that moment, she decided to honor her grandfather's legacy, take care of the cabin, and prove herself worthy of living there.

A few days later, she sat down with the foraging book. If she was going to survive alone in the mountains, there was much to learn. Although she had gathered berries and other edibles during her time with Morten, there were still many plants she didn't recognize. The book was well-organized, outlining which plants grew in the mountains and which could only be found in the lowlands: rowan berries, roseroot, crowberries, watercress, dandelion, birch leaves, yarrow, wild garlic—the list of edible plants was endless.

Fortunately, the book also detailed how to use and prepare each plant. Some were best pickled, others dried, some cooked, and some could be eaten raw. A whole new world of exciting possibilities opened up, and Maja found a sense of purpose in dedicating herself to exploring nature's wild and flavorful plants.

In those early years, she tried and failed often, but eventually, she discovered favorites, like tea brewed from dried nettles, dandelion, and birch leaves. The taste was a bit bitter, so she experimented with sweeter plants. Clover turned out to add just the right amount of sweetness, and she began to enjoy the refreshing drink daily.

As her knowledge expanded and she settled into her new life in the cabin, Maja also explored the fjords down in the lowlands. At least twice each summer, she took her fishing rod to one of the nearby deserted fjord branches along the Sognefjord. Most of the time, she was lucky enough to catch a cod or two, but seaweed was her main target. According to the book, several edible species of seaweed could be found along the Norwegian coast. She collected plenty of bladderwrack, which she sun-dried and ground into a spice, adding a natural salty flavor to both cod and mountain trout.

Even though her grandfather had wanted her to get a proper education, that path had never been meant for her. After his death, she couldn't focus on school. The job as a waitress had suited her just fine, and when she married Morten and he wanted her to stay at home, she was okay with that too.

But now, life in the mountains—the struggle for survival—had become her study. She dedicated her life to it. What the future held, she didn't know. With each passing day that no one discovered her, she felt more certain that it was her destiny to live and die alone in Didriksbu.

The year 2020 has just begun, and Maja decides that her grandfather's words should not be in vain. She owes him that much.

Knut

2020

A pandemic has turned the world upside down, and even a small country like Norway is heavily affected. The entire nation suddenly and brutally shuts down. For weeks, people must manage as best they can in their homes. New laws, COVID restrictions, limited office access, and layoffs define the new daily life for police officer Knut Langholm.

In the midst of this turbulence, Knut gets the chance to take some long-awaited vacation. But there's nowhere to go; everyone must stay within their own county, and restrictions limit any plans he might have.

Fortunately, nature is open, so he decides to head to the mountains in Stølsheimen.

"The DNT cabins are closed, of course, but a tent will do," he thinks.

While retrieving his outdoor gear from the storage room, Knut stumbles upon the old sardine cans. He had always meant to visit the Bjørn West Museum to see if these cans could be linked to the resistance movement in the mountains. Now that the museum is closed, he decides to call and see if anyone can look into it.

A friendly woman answers, and Knut explains the find as best he can. She suggests that he leave the box of canned goods outside the museum, and they will investigate further. After packing the car, he drives north toward Matre and the Bjørn West Museum.

The small village, mostly made up of the museum, a marine research institute, some homes, a school, a kindergarten, and the power company's installations, is nestled at the innermost part of Matrefjorden, surrounded by towering mountains. The sun disappears for several months each winter.

For Knut, the place feels claustrophobic, and he eagerly anticipates driving up into the higher, more open landscapes. Disappointed that he can't visit the museum or meet the curator, Borghild Matre, in person, he leaves the box of sardines on the museum's steps.

Before leaving, he reads some of the history of Bjørn West on the signs outside the museum. It's strange to think that battles were fought in the mountains, and that many people died in areas where he now loves to hike.

The drive up to Stordalen is as spectacular as ever—waterfalls, steep mountains, deep valleys, and the narrow, winding road with sharp turns that leads up from the valley floor. Knut never quite gets used to the overhanging cliffs, which look like they could break loose at any moment, crashing down to crush him and the car.

Once at the top, he breathes a sigh of relief—it went well this time too. As before, he drives down the long gravel road to Stølsvatnet. He packs his backpack and sets off. His goal is to follow the same route as last time, past the spot where he found the sardine cans, but this time to venture further into new, unknown trails in the mountains. He's skilled with maps and compasses, and he has enough food for several days. If he catches any fish, he might extend his stay.

He spends the first night near the spot where the car was found. With no luck fishing, he settles for freeze-dried spaghetti Bolognese for dinner. The food is quite tasty, but of course, it doesn't compare to freshly fried trout from his own rod.

The next day, he continues toward Nystølen and Sponga Lake, a nearby fishing spot. That evening, lying in his sleeping bag, he reflects on how lucky he is to experience such moments. Life as a police officer is demanding, with lots of overtime. The days blur into an endless stream of paperwork, with constant demands on his attention. His thoughts drift to Solveig, the young girl he has been in regular contact with. He feels sorry for her and wishes he could do more to help. It's clear that something isn't right at home, but without anyone asking for help, the police can't intervene. Knut sighs heavily, turns over in his sleeping bag, and soon falls asleep.

On the third day, he decides to navigate using his map and compass. His training with the Red Cross as a young man had taught him survival, first aid, and navigation skills—valuable knowledge he's used many times in his police work. Today, he aims for a small peak where he hopes to get a nice view of the Sognefjord. He sets his compass and heads off.

The terrain is steep and rugged, but occasionally, he finds smooth rocky areas where walking is easier. After a while, he sits down for lunch—flatbread with tube cheese. After eating, he lies down in the heather and falls asleep.

He wakes suddenly to the sound of movement in the nearby bushes. Slowly, he sits up, trying to locate the source of the sound. To his right, there's a steep slope with low pine trees, and that's where he sees her.

Gracefully, she climbs the steep slope, moving inch by inch, using the tree branches and balancing lightly on the small outcrops of the rock face. It's like watching a mountain goat—her movements are so effortless that she seems to blend into the landscape. If it weren't for her pink cap and the glimpse of light hair, Knut might have thought he was seeing things.

She disappears over the ridge, and Knut wonders where she went. According to the map, there's nothing but a steep scree on the other side. Curious, he packs up his things and takes a different route to the spot where she vanished. At the top of the ridge, he looks out over another valley—nothing but scree as far as the eye can see.

"She must have continued on the other side," he thinks. "There's no way to get down here." Puzzled, he decides to head in the opposite direction.

That evening, light drizzle falls as Knut eats dinner comfortably inside his tent. His thoughts return to the figure in the scree. Could he have imagined it? It's rare for him to meet other people when he strays from the main DNT trails. Perhaps it's the same woman he encountered at Vardadalsbu years ago—the one who gave a false name. He remembers she had the same light pink cap. He chuckles at himself, remembering how he'd written in the cabin logbook that he hoped to see her again. The thought is almost embarrassing now. But back then, just as now, he was captivated. The romantic in him can't help but dream of someday meeting a girl in the mountains who loves the outdoors as much as he does.

The next morning, the sun is shining, and Knut decides to head back to the car. Along the way, he takes a longer break, hoping to check for cell service. As soon as 4G appears on his phone, his inbox pings. An email from Borghild Matre catches his attention, asking him to call her.

Intrigued, he dials the number she provided.

"Hello, this is Borghild," she answers after just two rings.

"Hi, this is Knut Langholm, the guy with the sardine cans," he replies with a light tone.

"Oh, great! I'm so glad you called. The gift you left on the museum steps turned out to be quite interesting," she says enthusiastically. "I've done some research, and the answer might surprise you. The cans most likely have nothing to do with Bjørn West. After speaking with Erling Ravneberg, the last surviving veteran, we're confident that sardines weren't included in any parachute drops from England. Nor were they a common provision for the soldiers."

"That's odd," Knut replies. "Who on earth would haul sardine cans up into the mountains?"

"Ravneberg mentioned something else," Borghild continues. "There was a rumor that surfaced years after the war—someone supposedly planned to build a supply depot in a hidden location up in the mountains. Whether it was a private individual or, as Ravneberg suggested, the authorities, it's intriguing. It's possible they were preparing for another potential conflict. There's a lot of classified information from that time."

"Wow, that's really interesting," Knut says, his curiosity piqued. "I'll definitely do some digging when I get back to work. Thanks for the tip. Let me know if you find out anything else."

After the call ends, Knut sits in silence, deep in thought. A mystery in the mountains isn't something to be dismissed lightly—perhaps he has stumbled upon a well-kept, post-war secret?

Before long, he is back at his car. Although he had planned to camp for another night, the new information drove him to return to his apartment in Knarvik. The investigator in him is triggered; he needs to dig deeper into this.

The next day, working from home as the office is still closed, Knut sits down at his computer. He doesn't expect to find state secrets through a simple Google search, but he wants to see if anything about hidden supply depots in Norway is accessible. Sure enough, he finds a number of references to secret cabins and hidden hideaways, scattered throughout Norway's mountains and forests. The idea of someone building a secret stash in Stølsheimen isn't far-fetched.

"But it must have been private," he thinks.

Before he can delve deeper, his phone rings. It is his colleague, Preben Knudsen, also working from home.

"Hey, Preben, how's working from home treating you?" Knut jokes. "I hear rumors that you're only wearing boxers under the desk—shirt and tie just for show."

Preben laughs and stands up, showing off his colorful boxers.

"You nailed it. No point dressing up more than necessary."

They both chuckle before Preben gets serious.

"But listen, something came up that I think you'll want to know. It's about that car case—the woman who committed suicide in the mountain lake. It turns out she had another car registered in her name—a blue Opel station wagon from 1987."

"Okay," Knut says, intrigued. "And has that car turned up in a lake somewhere too?"

"Not quite, but it's strange. The car's license plate was recorded twice at the toll station near Voss—once in the spring of 2016 and again just a few days ago. No transponder, just the plate. A bill was sent, but no one paid."

Knut's curiosity deepens. "Could the family have kept the car? Maybe there's nothing mysterious about it."

"Possibly, but the car was previously registered to an Ingvar Sandnes, who lived on a property in Masfjordnes," Preben says. "It might be nothing, but I thought you'd want to look into it."

"Good thinking. That case has always felt off—the daughters are struggling to accept that their mother took her own life. Without a body, they're holding on to the hope that she's still alive."

Knut thanks Preben and asks him to forward the toll details. The car had passed through the toll station twice, once in 2016 and again just a few days ago, with no other records in between. He decides to investigate the property in Masfjordnes.

A quick search reveals that Maja, the woman who disappeared, owned the land, which included three buildings: a main house, a guest house, and a barn. A law firm in Bergen is listed as the administrator. When Knut calls the firm, he learns that Maja's daughter, Solveig, is the heir to everything—including the old Opel in the barn. The paperwork is still in process, which explains why the name change hasn't been registered yet. It is possible that Solveig had used the car, accounting for the toll in 2020—but what about 2016?

Knut makes a fresh pot of coffee, feeling the need to talk to Solveig, but not before gathering more information. She is still vulnerable, and he doesn't want to stir up false hope.

Back at his computer, Knut searches for more about Ingvar Sandnes. Soon, a photo of an older man appears on a memorial site. Ingvar had been involved in the early development of the water systems in Stølsheimen and Matre, a skilled engineer who contributed significantly over the years. Sadly, he passed away from cancer in 2000. His obituary mentions he was survived by one grandchild—Maja.

The next image that comes up makes Knut even more interested. It shows a young boy dressed in a Home Guard uniform. When he clicks on the link, it takes him to the Bjørn West Museum's homepage. He quickly finds information about a soldier named Ingvar Sandnes, who had been wounded by the Germans in the mountains at just seventeen years old, and how he had managed to survive. After lying cold and alone in an old shed for an entire week, he was found by his own grandfather and brought home to the farm at Masfjordnes.

A thought begins to form in Knut's mind, but he can't quite grasp it. Is there a connection here that he isn't seeing? Could Ingvar's hiding place have something to do with the sardine cans? As an engineer and former soldier, he must have been a knowledgeable man with many talents. But that still doesn't explain who drove the car in 2016.

The law firm mentioned that the guest house on the property had been rented out from time to time, but no one had lived there since 2014, when the last tenant, a young student teacher, moved out. So, it couldn't have been a tenant who borrowed the car without permission. Could it have been a neighbor or someone else with access to the main house?

Knut logs into the land registry and finds the deed to the property. No other owners are listed; the deed is solely in Maja Sandnes's name. But at the bottom of the last page, it is written in black and white: The property includes a twenty-hectare area in the northwestern part of the Stølsheimen mountains, Masfjorden municipality.

"This must be the connection I've been looking for," he thinks. It can't be anyone other than Ingvar Sandnes behind the rumor of a secret supply depot in the mountains. But rumors are just rumors—there is still more to uncover. Knut realizes it is time to involve Solveig in these new discoveries and begins typing a message to her.

"We need to talk. Can we meet somewhere as soon as possible? Knut."

Before he can send the message, a shiver runs through him. He finally remembers who the woman with the false name he met at Vardadalsbu nearly ten years ago reminded him of.

Solveig

2020

The year 2020 starts off well for Solveig. She has come up with a viable plan, and now all that remains is to put it into action. She is still uncertain about how to proceed, but she decides to try talking to Kjersti. It has been a long time since they talked, just the two of them.

One afternoon in late February, she gets the chance. Her dad is working late, the boys are at soccer practice, and Laura is visiting a friend—it's just her and Kjersti at home.

"Come and sit on the couch with me for a bit, please," she says to Kjersti. "I need to talk to you about something."

Suddenly, she gets cold feet. What if Kjersti tells her dad? Maybe she shouldn't reveal everything, just part of the truth. She decides on the latter.

"You're like a mother to me and Laura. I think Mom would have appreciated that," she begins. "But it's been incredibly difficult to watch how Dad has bossed you around all these years. You're worth so much more, and he doesn't deserve you."

Kjersti gently smooths some hair behind her ears and sighs softly before turning to Solveig.

"Life isn't always easy for any of us. Your dad has his challenges too. I know he doesn't mean any harm; he had a difficult childhood," she says quietly. "Yes, maybe I've let him boss us around and make all the decisions, but we have a roof over our heads and food on the table—we lack nothing, and that's worth something too."

Solveig had expected Kjersti to defend her father and realizes that this is going to be difficult. It's not just a matter of convincing her to leave him.

"When school ends, I'm going to move, and I want you and the younger kids to come with me," Solveig says. "I inherited a place from Mom—there's room for all of us."

The words are out; there is no turning back now. She can only hope for the best.

"That's exciting, I'm happy for you. But my place is here. With him. You know what will happen—he'll just come after me and convince me to move back. I'm weak, you know that, but at the same time, I'm stronger than you think," Kjersti replies, taking Solveig's hands in hers. "You and your sister are as dear to me as my own two rascals, but despite everything, I love your father, and my place is with him."

Persuasion is useless, Solveig realizes. Her father has Kjersti in the palm of his hand—the ties are strong despite the violence and daily humiliations. All she can hope for is that Laura will come with her. When the time comes, she will stand up to her father and fight back.

Just a few weeks later, the opportunity she has been

waiting for comes, but much earlier than she had planned. The pandemic that started far away in China has reached Norway, and both she and her siblings have to attend school from home. No one knows how long it will last.

"Dad is going to be home too. The whole family stuck together for weeks under the same roof—it's a recipe for disaster," she thinks.

Solveig couldn't have been more right. It takes just a few days for all hell to break loose. The boys are restless and find it difficult to deal with school at home. Soccer practice is canceled. Laura mostly stays in her room doing homework or listening to music. Morten uses the living room as his home office and snaps at anyone who makes noise or disturbs him. Everyone's patience is worn thin, and Kjersti has it the worst, expected to keep the house in order, prepare all the meals, and still remain invisible. She tiptoes around, but nothing is good enough for the tyrant who has taken over the living room.

"Do you have to sneak around like that?" he yells sharply at her. "You're everywhere, making noise all the time. How do you expect me to get anything done? You can't even control the boys—they're slamming doors and wandering in and out constantly."

Kjersti is shoved by an elbow that holds her in a chokehold; the thud against the wall echoes through the house. The boys retreat to their room—they know they stand no chance when their father is in this mood. Solveig would usually keep her distance, too, but now she can't take it anymore—this has to stop.

She positions herself by her father and screams as loud as she can,

"Stop! You're going to kill her."

Her father releases Kjersti, who collapses onto the floor. He turns toward Solveig and lands a punch directly in her face. The blow is swift and brutal—she doesn't stand a chance of dodging it. The pain overwhelms her, and she curls up to protect herself from further blows.

"You don't speak to me like that. I demand respect from my own children, just as I had to respect my father. You're just as insolent and useless as your mother," he says coldly.

Morten gives her two hard kicks in the back before storming out. Shortly after, they hear the screeching tires of the car speeding away from the house.

Laura emerges, terrified, from her room.

"Get my phone," Solveig whispers. Laura does as she's told.

With trembling hands, Solveig finds Knut's number. He answers on the first ring.

"Can you come? Dad broke my nose and tried to kill Kjersti," she says, her voice slurred.

Not long after, they hear the sirens of a police car. Knut comes in through the door with two police officers right behind him. He takes a quick look around and asks Laura where her father is. She tells him that he drove off just before the police arrived.

"Chase after him and put out a radio alert," he says to

one of the other officers. "Get an ambulance too."

Knut checks on Kjersti first. She is in obvious pain and struggling to breathe.

"Hang in there—the ambulance will be here soon," he says, helping her into a more comfortable position, lying on her side. Then he checks on Solveig.

"You took a hard hit, but I don't think your nose is broken," he reassures her. "Are you hurt anywhere else?"

"My back—he kicked me twice," she sobs. "But I'm okay. I stood up to him, and he didn't like that."

"That was very brave of you, and it's good that you called. He won't be able to talk his way out of this; he'll have to face the consequences of his violence," he says, gently stroking her arm.

Soon, the house is full of police and paramedics. Kjersti is carried away on a stretcher and taken to Haukeland Hospital in Bergen with full sirens. Solveig is also sent to the hospital; they need to take X-rays to determine if her nose is broken or not.

"What about the boys and Laura?" she says to Knut. "They can't stay here alone—what if Dad comes back?"

"Don't worry about that—we'll take care of them and keep watch all night," Knut replies. "If he shows up, he'll be arrested."

Solveig and Kjersti spend the night at the hospital. Kjersti's larynx was severely damaged, and she needs help breathing. They plan to keep her under observation for a few more days.

But Solveig is allowed to go home the next day.

She is picked up by a police patrol after the doctor approves her discharge.

At home, she is greeted by Knut, who is making breakfast. The atmosphere is relaxed, and Laura and the boys are chatting away.

"Wouldn't it be wonderful if we could have such a pleasant time around the breakfast table every day?" Solveig thinks.

"Hey, how are you doing?" Knut asks while flipping a pancake onto Laura's plate. "As you can see, you didn't need to worry about these three—they're managing just fine. Want a pancake too?"

"My nose isn't broken, thankfully, but I have to take it easy for a few days because of two fractured ribs," Solveig replies. "Yes, I'd like a pancake. Has there been any sign of Dad?"

"It seems he's figured out that we're here, so no, he's stayed away. All units are on the lookout for his car, but so far, it's like he's disappeared," Knut responds. "But sooner or later, he'll likely show up. We'll stay here as long as needed."

"Good. By the way, there's something I want to talk to you about—maybe we can discuss it after break-fast?" Solveig suggests.

"Of course, I've got something to tell you too," Knut replies.

A while later, after breakfast has been eaten, the dishes cleared, and the younger kids have gone to their rooms for online classes, Solveig sits down and tells

Knut everything that has happened since she found out about the inheritance and her visit to the property in Masfjorden.

"I've decided to move there. I had hoped Kjersti and the kids would come with me, but convincing her seems impossible. It almost seems like she's excusing Dad's behavior—she actually blames herself. Why is she like that?" Solveig asks.

"People who live in abusive relationships are often manipulated into believing that they are the ones at fault. The abusers are usually psychopaths who know exactly how to control their partners," Knut explains. "Convincing them to press charges is often impossible. I'm afraid your mother experienced abuse too—she never reported him either."

Solveig thinks about his answer for a long time but still finds it hard to accept.

"This time he went too far, and I hope Kjersti agrees to press charges. I'm going to do it, at least. Will it be enough to get him jailed?" she asks.

"Yes, absolutely. The assault on you carries a prison sentence of up to six years," Knut replies. "By the way, when you visited the property in Masfjorden, did you find a car in the barn?"

"No, I didn't go inside the barn—just the two houses," Solveig says, looking curiously at him. "How do you know there's a car there?"

"The license plate came up during the search for your mother's car. It turns out she had another car, which is very likely in the barn at Masfjordnes. But the strange thing is, it was registered at the toll station just before Voss in 2016 and again just a few weeks ago. It would make sense if it was you who used it recently, but it's a mystery who drove it in 2016," he says. "Does anyone else know about the property?"

"Not that I know of. Dad never mentioned Masfjordnes, and I haven't told anyone," she replies. Then a thought strikes her, and she looks at Knut with wide eyes. "Do you think it could be Mom? Could she still be alive?"

"I don't want to get your hopes up—it's more likely to be some kids or a neighbor who was up to something, but there's another strange thing I need to tell you. Several years ago, long after your mother disappeared, I was on a hiking trip in Stølsheimen. The first night, I stayed in one of the DNT cabins, specifically Vardadalsbu. When I walked in, I was greeted by a frightened woman who barely spoke a word to me. She left quickly after that. The name she wrote in the logbook, Kristine Fjellstad, doesn't exist. The feeling that I had seen her before has stayed with me all these years, and now with your mother's case and rumors about a supply cache in the mountains coming up, it struck me that this woman reminded me suspiciously of your mother," Knut explains. "I did meet her once, back when I was at your house."

Solveig can hardly believe what she is hearing. Could it be possible that her mother is alive and has been hiding all these years?

"What do you mean about a supply cache in the mountains?" she asks.

"I've discovered that a large area in Stølsheimen belongs to the farm you've inherited, and that your great-grandfather was a soldier in the Bjørn West guerrilla group during World War II. He was wounded by a German bullet and hid in an old mountain cabin for several days before his grandfather brought him home," Knut explains. "A connection isn't unlikely."

Solveig stands up, goes to her room, retrieves the photo where she had discovered the coordinates, and hands it to Knut.

"Could it be here? I found this picture in Mom's album," she says hopefully.

Knut enters the coordinates into his phone. The map that appears shows an area that doesn't belong to Stølsheimen or any of the places where the soldiers had been. Disappointed, Solveig sits down in the chair again.

"Oh, shoot, I totally forgot," she says, running back to her room. She returns with a key. "I got this from the lawyers. It fits a safety deposit box at Sparebanken in Knarvik. I was supposed to retrieve the contents but haven't gotten around to it yet. Do you think we could go and check?" she asks hopefully.

"That's the best lead I've seen in a long time. Yes, let's go investigate—I'll ask a colleague to come here and replace me, then we can head out," he answers.

An hour later, they are on their way to the bank in Knarvik. Due to COVID-19 restrictions, the bank is closed to customers, but Knut uses his status as chief inspector, and the bank manager himself meets them at the door.

"The vault is down here," he says, leading them down a staircase inside the bank.

It is cold in the basement, and Solveig shivers for a moment. The tension is palpable as she takes out the key and inserts it into the lock of box number 232. The bank manager inserts his duplicate key, and together they open the compartment where a black box has lain untouched for several years.

"My mother was the last person to handle this box," Solveig thinks as she carefully lifts it out. The bank manager and Knut turn away, giving her a private moment—it is, after all, her inheritance.

A single envelope is the only thing inside the box. On the outside, her mother's neat handwriting reads:

"To my daughters, Solveig and Laura."

Solveig takes the envelope with her as she leaves. The time has come to involve her sister; this letter is for both of them.

Back at the house, Solveig goes into Laura's room. After about an hour, they come out, both with red-rimmed eyes. In the living room, Knut sits waiting anxiously.

"Is there anything you want to share with me?" he asks kindly.

Solveig takes out the letter and begins to read.

LISE K. VIKEN

To my beloved daughters,

If you're reading this, it means I'm no longer with you. Without knowing what has happened, other than that I hopefully died of old age, happily surrounded by children, grandchildren, and great-grandchildren, there is something I must share with you. Every family has its secrets. Our little family is no exception. I don't know the whole story myself, and perhaps I'll never know it either, but when my grandfather died, he left behind a backpack. It wasn't until a year after his death that I opened it. Inside, I found various survival gear and a map with some coordinates. Just before he passed away, Grandpa told me there was a place I could go if the world ended or if life went wrong. There, I would find food and supplies to last for many years. No one knows about this secret. All I know is that the cabin is called Didriksbu and it's located in Stølsheimen. The coordinates are the only clue he left behind. I've never been there myself, at least not yet.

Now, this is your inheritance, and I leave it to you to either check out the place or do as I did—hide the backpack with the gear somewhere safe and take it out if it ever becomes necessary to evacuate. I've memorized the coordinates before placing them here in the box with the letter, to make sure they didn't fall into the wrong hands. Take care of each other and use the inheritance wisely. Remember, you are always in my heart—I love you forever.
Mom

For the first time in his life, Knut is speechless.

"My goodness. What a story. This is absolutely incredible," he says, amazed. "Could it be that the rumor that circulated many, many years ago is true? Does Didriksbu really exist?"

"We'd like to go there and investigate, and we hope you can come with us," Solveig says to Knut. "Of course, we have high expectations—we hope to find Mom—but if it turns out that she's there, it could mean that she ran away from all of us on purpose. Or that she actually tried to kill us."

"There are many unanswered questions, and I agree with you—we should go there and investigate. I know where we need to go," Knut says, recalling the woman he saw in the mountains a few days ago, the one who disappeared without a trace over the hilltop—it could have been Maja.

"But we have to wait until you're better, Solveig. I'll check with the hospital about when Kjersti can come home to the boys, and also arrange police protection for them. We'll leave when everything is ready."

Maja

2020

Maja is on her way back to the cabin with the second bag after another shopping trip to Voss in her grandfather's old car. As she climbs up the last steep slope, she senses more than sees the person emerging from the grass on the other side of the valley.

"Don't panic," she says to herself. "Just keep going and act like nothing's wrong."

And so she does. She moves easily and gracefully to the top, where she quickly hurries across and down the rocky slope. Maja quickly slips into safety, fairly certain that she wasn't noticed. She takes out her binoculars and peers through a small vent at the top of the entrance. Not long after, a person appears at the top. Her heart skips a beat—what if he comes down the slope? But the person just stands there for a long time, giving Maja time to take another look at him. There is something familiar about the figure. Then she realizes —it's the man she met a long time ago at Vardadalsbu.

He gazes out over the landscape before slowly turning around and leaving the area. Maja breathes a sigh of relief; that was really close. She has to pull herself together and be more careful the next time.

A whole week passes before Maja is ready for another trip to the storage at Stølsvatnet. The hiking season has just begun, the snow disappeared early this spring, and there are always people in the mountains. She has to be more cautious. Although she got a scare when Knut almost discovered the cabin, she has to admit that it was nice to see a familiar face. She has thought a lot about what it would be like to return to normal life.

The drive to Voss this time gave her a good sense of what it was like to be among people again. Even though she didn't talk to anyone and the streets were fairly empty, it felt nice to be part of society. Maja wondered a bit why most of the shops were closed, considering it was just a regular weekday. Even the grocery stores were quiet. The headlines in the newspapers gave her the answer. A pandemic called COVID-19 had spread across the world. The disease was causing death and devastation, but so far, there hadn't been many deaths in Norway.

The news came as a shock to Maja.

"Grandpa was really ahead of his time. It was precisely for situations like this that the cabin was built," she thought. No reason to wish to return to civilization, then—it seemed like she was safest in the mountains right now.

It is early morning when Maja arrives at Stølsvatnet. A tent is set up at the campsite near the dam, and there are two cars parked there, so she takes a wide detour to avoid being seen. Everything is quiet and calm; the people in the tent are still asleep. She sneaks into the cabin unnoticed. Her backpack is filled to the brim with dry goods. She takes her time to ensure the coast is clear before she locks up and starts on the same path back.

Dawn breaks, and the sun rises. Maja feels its warmth on both her body and soul. She has plenty of time, so when she stops for breakfast and lies down on a blanket in the heather, it doesn't take long before she falls asleep. It's only after several hours that she wakes up. Dazed, she looks around, taking a moment to remember where she is. Then she stretches her body to loosen her stiff muscles, puts the blanket back in her backpack, and continues the journey back to the cabin.

She climbs the last stone steps in the rocky terrain to Didriksbu. Then she stops abruptly. The door to the cabin, which is hidden until you get quite close, is slightly ajar.

"What on earth?" she thinks. "Did I forget to close it? That has never happened before. Or is someone here? Could it be Knut, back to investigate where I disappeared to?"

Her thoughts swirl as she slowly approaches the entrance. Just before she opens the door, she hears Doffen purring loudly. Calmly, she steps inside and takes a few seconds to let her eyes adjust to the darkness. Then she sees him. The man sitting in the rocking chair, with Doffen on his lap. But he's not Knut. The person who has entered the cabin is her ex-husband, Morten.

"Morten, is it really you? You're alive," Maja gasps. "I thought you were dead, gone forever."

The shock is so great that she has trouble speaking. She has to pinch her arm to make sure she isn't seeing things. But she isn't—he's there, and he's talking to her.

"And here you are. Hidden away in this cave. Did you really think no one would find you?" he says, calmly looking at her.

The cat curls up in his lap, completely unbothered by the fact that the man has risen from the dead.

"But how? The fire, the house burned down.

The girls—don't tell me they're alive too?" she asks, feeling her pulse quicken. Could it be?

"Yes, things didn't go exactly as you planned. We weren't home when you decided to kill us, but rest assured, you won't escape the charges of attempted murder," he says coldly.

The words hit her like a whip, but all Maja can think about is that her daughters are alive. My God, she's been living with grief and misery all these years, and for what? It's unbelievable. This must be a dream, or maybe one of her nightmares.

"I didn't mean to set the fire. I can't remember doing it. The girls meant everything to me, you know that," she says desperately. He has to believe her.

"It wouldn't be the first time you forgot what you did. The psychopath in you came out all the time, you can't deny that," he says, laughing loudly. "But you were so easy to trigger. All it took was a few pills in your wine glass, and you drank it down happily."

She looks up, not quite understanding what he means, but then it hits her—it wasn't she who was to blame for everything that happened. Maja collapses onto the floor. The explanation for all the episodes she doesn't remember finally becomes clear to her.

It was him, not her, who had caused it all. The shadow is Morten. He had manipulated her into believing she was unstable and dangerous. How could she have been so blind?

"But what about the fire? I would never have done something like that," she says desperately.

Evil shines in his eyes as he slowly strokes Doffen's head.

"A stroke of bad luck, that. When I picked up the girls that afternoon, it was no trouble slipping a few pills into the wine glass on the kitchen counter. You had placed a crate of firewood in the hallway, wood you were going to burn in the fire pit later that evening. That our house burned down that same night might have been a coincidence. Impossible to prove one way or the other. But with your psychopathic background, it's entirely believable that you were the one who set it on fire," he says maliciously.

"But why? What did I ever do to you that you wanted to hurt me so badly? I loved you," she says, looking at him with wide eyes.

"Why? Well, let me tell you, you slowly suffocated me with your love. It became too much. And you were easy to manipulate, far too easy—it stopped being fun. But it was all your secrets that became the tipping point. When were you planning to tell me about this place? Or about the property worth millions?

Not to mention the stocks?" he says, exasperated.

"Did you really think I didn't know about all of it? Did you really think I didn't know about the backpack in the basement? But the money—you kept that well hidden. And now your daughter is doing the same, hiding the truth about everything she inherited, but I found the envelope, hidden in a drawer in her room. She's a disappointment, just like you."

His words slowly sink in. He never loved her. The whole relationship had been a lie. She had idolized him, but it had never been reciprocated. Even when he'd moved out, she had wanted him back. How naive she had been.

"Two miserable girls were all you could give me. All I ever wanted was a son, but you couldn't even do that. And you lied to me, told me we could try again, even though you knew it was too late,"

he says with a hurt voice.

"I'm sorry I didn't tell you that I couldn't have more children. I knew how disappointed you would be," she says in a thin voice. A small part of her is still vulnerable to his manipulation, and for a moment, she imagines that it's not too late for them to try again.

Morten suddenly stands up, and Doffen jumps down onto the floor. Then he grabs the back of Maja's head.

"You should be dead. Drowned in the lake. But here you are, alive and kicking, but don't think you can rise from the dead and come back to take everything from me. This ends here," he says, throwing her against the kitchen cabinet.

Helpless like a ragdoll, Maja feels him grab her again and drive a fist hard into her stomach. Then come more kicks, to her back and stomach, before he takes a small break.

"The girls don't need you. They've never missed you, and why would they? You're not worth keeping around, you worthless bitch," he hurls insults at her.

Her head is pounding, and her body is battered, but Maja manages to curl up and slowly crawl towards the bed. Just as he's about to grab her again, she manages to pull out the gun her grandfather had hidden behind a plank at the bed's base. Before she has time to think about what she's doing, she turns toward Morten and aims. The shot echoes like thunder inside the small cabin. Afterward, everything falls silent.

Meanwhile, a small delegation consisting of a grown man and two teenage girls is making its way toward the secret cabin. They have located the coordinates on the map, and the man in the group, Chief Inspector Knut Langholm, soon recognizes the area. It's the same place where he went camping just a few days ago. They are nearing the top of the steep, rocky slope where he saw a woman seemingly disappear into thin air. Suddenly, there's a loud bang, like a large stone has dislodged.

"Wait here, girls. I'm going down to investigate. It sounded like a gunshot," he says, turning to Solveig and Laura.

Solveig is in obvious pain from her back and carefully sits down. Nothing in the world could have stopped her from joining this expedition.

Knut moves cautiously down the rocky slope. One wrong step here, and he could easily trigger an avalanche. Halfway down, he pauses and looks around. To his right, there are some flat rocks not covered in moss. They seem to form a narrow staircase winding up through the scree. Carefully, he ascends, and soon he sees it: a small opening in the rocks and what looks like a wooden door. It's well hidden from the outside world and impossible to spot unless you know it's there. There are no sounds to be heard.

Slowly, he climbs the last steps and glances right and left into the antechamber, built from stones in the rocky slope. Then he pushes open the wooden door and steps inside. It takes his eyes a few minutes to adjust to the dim light, but the sight that meets him is something he will never forget.

On the floor lies Morten. A bullet has struck him in the stomach, and he is unconscious.

At the other end of the room, on the bed platform, sits Maja, still holding the gun. Her eyes are wide with shock. She doesn't seem to notice that someone else has entered the small cabin. Knut speaks softly to her as he approaches.

"Put the gun down, Maja. It's over," he whispers to her.

As if in a trance, she slowly turns to him and realizes who he is.

"It's you. You found me at last," she says, handing him the gun. She begins to cry, and Knut takes her into his arms. They sit like that for a long time, just holding each other.

"You're injured," he says.

"I'll be fine. This isn't the first time," she says bravely. "How did you know I was here?"

"It's a long story. I'll tell you another time. I brought two people with me who are eager to see you. They're waiting at the top of the slope. Do you think you can make it up there?"

"My girls? They're here? I thought they were dead, that I had killed them, but I couldn't have, could I? Morten says I did it, but all I wanted was to burn some wood that day." Maja's voice cracks; this is almost too much for her.

"Everything will come to light; I promise you. They're not dead; they're alive and well, and they never gave up hope that you would return," Knut replies. "Come, I'll help you."

He takes her by the arm and supports her as they exit the cabin. Slowly but surely, they approach the top, where Solveig and Laura have stood up and are moving toward the woman they barely recognize as the mother they've missed almost their entire lives.

Before he knows it, the mother and daughters are embracing each other. Tears stream down Knut's cheeks as he witnesses the emotional reunion. For twelve years, they have lived apart—two girls who didn't know what had happened to their mother, and a mother who had lived in solitude, burdened with guilt and pain over a lie. Nothing can separate them anymore; life has given them a second chance.

They are still clinging to each other when the sound of a helicopter is heard in the distance. Knut has called for assistance. Maja has a deep cut on her forehead, and she is in severe pain from her back. She needs medical attention. He is also worried about Solveig; the young girl hasn't complained once during the three-hour hike, but he noticed how she occasionally clutched her stomach and breathed heavily. And then there's Morten. He's lost a lot of blood and needs to be taken to the hospital.

The ambulance helicopter arrives first, and Knut helps Maja and the two girls safely aboard. Solveig and Laura never let go of Maja, as if they are terrified of losing her again. The medical personnel carry Morten, who is still unconscious, up from the scree and into the waiting helicopter.

Knut stands alone on the ground as the helicopter takes off and disappears over the mountain peaks. Then it's gone, and everything is silent. Not a breath of wind can be heard. He sits down on a rock and tries to process everything that has happened.

Half an hour later, the police helicopter lands, and together with the forensic technicians, he heads down to the cabin. They immediately begin documenting everything. Before they leave, Knut takes one last walk down to the stone hut. Reverently, he stands in the small room that Maja has used as both a living room and a bedroom.

"How in the world did you manage here for so long

without being discovered?" he says to the walls. "It takes enormous strength and courage; most would have given up after a short time. What are you made of?"

On the steps outside, he is met by Doffen. The little cat had disappeared during all the commotion, but now he's back, rubbing against Knut's legs.

"Hey there, where did you come from? Do you live here too?" he says, stroking the cat's back. "You'd better come along as well." Knut picks Doffen up in his arms, and together they head up to the waiting helicopter.

Epilogue

The rustling of the pine trees drowns out the sound of laughter coming from inside the house. Maja pauses for a moment, leans on her rake, and gazes out over the freshly mown meadow. The hay, which they stack in the traditional way, will be enough to sustain the two cows and the horse, Blakken, through the coming winter. Now, the three animals graze in the field behind the houses, where there is plenty of fresh, juicy grass that they quietly munch on. Over by the barn, there's new life in the chicken coop. Four hens and a feisty rooster strut around inside the enclosure.

Every morning, one of the children runs over to check if any eggs have been laid. They've even made a chart to see who can find the most eggs in a week. She chuckles to herself; they are all wonderful, her two beloved daughters, but also Kjersti's fine boys, the girls' half-brothers, whom she has already grown fond of.

Today marks exactly two years since her life was once again turned upside down. The happiness and gratitude she feels—from living a lonely life, condemned to eternal exile, to finding her way back to her grandfather's beloved farm in Masfjordnes, surrounded by people who wish her well—feels like nothing short of a miracle to Maja.

If it hadn't been for her grandfather's pistol, she dares

not think about what might have happened.

Perhaps Knut would have arrived in time; but even if he had, it's not certain he could have stopped Morten from killing her.

The first months after returning to civilization, she had nightmares every night, waking up drenched in sweat. The moment she fired the pistol haunted her. It wasn't until several months later, when the court ruled that she had acted in self-defense, that she was able to rid herself of the disturbing images in her head. Shooting another person, even in self-defense, felt quite traumatic.

Of course, it was a shock to Kjersti and the children to discover that she was alive and had shot Morten. But after the whole story came out—how Morten had systematically drugged her for years, even after he had moved out—they gradually came to accept it.

Knut had been a great support to all of them during those early days, but perhaps most of all to Maja. He helped her regain her life. She had to go through a bureaucratic maze to "rise from the dead," and she had to regain custody of Laura.

When Maja disappeared, Morten had automatically gained custody. And when he married Kjersti, she had adopted both girls and become their official mother. The old diagnosis of psychopathy was brought up, and the judge in the case was concerned about Maja's health. A new evaluation was conducted.

The psychiatrist who examined her found no signs of psychopathic traits.

Knut decided to look more closely into the previous diagnosis, and what he discovered shocked them all. It turned out that the doctor Morten had taken her to had been dismissed many years ago. Repeated misdiagnoses, bribes, and suspicion of corruption were listed as reasons for his dismissal. With this information as a backdrop, the judge completely reversed the previous ruling and granted Maja full custody. In court, he even went so far as to apologize for everything she had been through, acknowledging that the strain imposed by the court had been an additional burden.

Although both girls would soon be of age, it meant the world to Maja to have her name on paper as their primary caregiver and mother.

Sometimes she's overwhelmed when she thinks about all the years they've lost—birthdays, confirmations, school graduations, football games. Not to mention all the breakfasts, dinners, goodnight hugs, and homework help around the dinner table. No, she can hardly bear to think about it.

They had to get to know each other again. Laura was just a little girl when Maja disappeared and doesn't remember much. But the longing for her real mother had always been there, and now that Maja is back in her life, she can hardly bear to let her out of sight, terrified that she might leave again. Solveig, who has already grown up, has become like a friend. The two of them have talked a lot about life, joys, and sorrows. During one of their conversations, it came out that it was Solveig she had seen that time on the football field in Voss. To think that Maja had sat just a few meters from her own daughter and didn't realize it was her! How random and unfair life could be sometimes.

After the doctors patched up Morten, he was transferred to Bergen prison. The charges against him were serious: attempted murder, rape, years of abuse, drugging, and psychological violence, all carrying heavy sentences. The trial against him lasted for several months and was a significant ordeal for Maja and the girls, who all had to testify.

A visibly broken Morten was unable to look her in the eye when it was Maja's turn to take the witness stand. She answered all the questions as best she could, and when she testified about the rape, Morten broke down, sobbing quietly.

When the sentence was announced, everyone breathed a sigh of relief. Twelve years behind bars. Finally, they were free from the man who had caused so much pain.

Kjersti comes out into the yard. The woman with the long blonde hair, whom Maja had once hated when she was poisoned by darkness. The side effects of the drugs, Morten had given her over the years, had caused her to have blackouts for short periods. It took her time to come to terms with that realization. The psychologist she still sees once a month has helped her see things in the right perspective. She owes her life to Kjersti. It was she who stepped up and took care of her daughters. For that, she is eternally grateful.

"I've asked the boys to bring the garden furniture from the barn," says Kjersti, giving Maja a hug. "They solemnly promised to put away their iPads."

Kjersti was skeptical of Maja at first. Morten had fed her all kinds of lies and bad-mouthed her at every opportunity. It was as if Kjersti also believed Maja was crazy.

After the trial was over, they had sat down at a café to talk. For over three hours, they discussed everything that had happened. The bond between them was strong —their children were siblings, and they agreed to do everything they could to ensure the kids wouldn't be permanently damaged by everything that had happened. Splitting up the siblings seemed absurd, and when Maja suggested that Kjersti and the boys could live in the small house on the farm in Masfjordnes, while she and the girls took the main house, they both burst into tears of joy. They couldn't have found a better solution.

The kids quickly settled into Sandnes School, and Solveig took the bus back and forth to Knarvik High School every day. Sometimes she borrowed the old car that great-grandfather Ingvar had owned, simply because the car was so old and ugly that her classmates thought it was cool.

Doffen also got company from two orphaned kittens they had taken in. Like most cats, he took life easy and quickly settled into his new home. But it was still Maja he turned to when he needed affection. Then he would meow, jump into her lap, and demand to be scratched under the chin. It was as if he was saying,

"You're really just mine."

The story of the woman who had hidden in the mountains for twelve years made big news. The media devoured the case, with daily updates on everything from how she had tried to kill her children to stories about her supposed psychopathy diagnosis. The phone rang incessantly. Eventually, she had to stop answering.

For the sake of the children and all their friends, she finally agreed to do a longer interview with *Bergens Tidende*. There, she was able to explain how everything fit together, and the journalist did an excellent job of portraying her as the person she really was.

After the article was published, she received many kind and positive responses, from people who had dreamed of doing something similar and women who had found strength in her story and managed to break free from abusive husbands. Recently, Maja accepted an offer from a major publisher to write a book about her experiences.

Although she dreads delving into all the events, her psychologist has advised her to go through with it. To truly reclaim her life, she must put the past behind her.

Maja sets down the rake and goes into the house. The girls are busy baking buns—it's Saturday, and they've planned a picnic in the garden.

"You're doing a great job," she praises them. "Did

you take out the raspberries from the freezer for the jam?"

After settling in Masfjordnes, Maja had continued to live off the land as much as she could. The previous fall, they had cleared the area around the raspberry bushes that Ingvar had planted many years ago. They were still full of large, delicious berries, which everyone had helped pick. They had already eaten the jars of jam they had made, but there were still a few boxes of frozen berries left, saved for occasions like this.

"We did, Mom. We'll mash them with sugar as soon as we get the buns in the oven," says Laura, giving her a hug.

She strokes her daughter's cheek—the indescribably good feeling of being called 'Mom' cannot be put into words. She can hardly believe that life has granted her such happiness. And in a few months, the new life just beginning to grow in her belly will make her life complete. For now, only she and Knut know about it. The plan is to share the good news later in the day when everyone is gathered for the picnic.

"Great, it won't be long before they get here. I'll go help the boys with the garden furniture," she says, and heads back outside.

In the time following what she called the homecoming, Knut had visited them almost every day. It was Kjersti who made Maja aware that he had taken a liking to her.

"Don't you see the way he looks at you?" she said

one afternoon when they had taken a break from renovating the old farmhouse. "He practically devours you with his eyes."

Maja laughed. She hadn't noticed, but she liked the idea. A few days later, she had been outside inspecting the old, green-painted bench that her grandfather Ingvar had made for his beloved Kristine. The plaque with the inscription *Because I Love You* had become illegible over the years. Knut appeared beside her.

"Hey, I didn't hear you arrive," she said with a smile. "Would you like to hear the story of this old, worn bench?" He said he would, and Maja told him about her grandfather, who had been cheeky enough to promise Kristine a green-painted bench before they were even properly dating.

"Pretty romantic, don't you think?" Maja said, turning toward him. Knut looked deeply into her eyes, and for a moment, she nearly lost her breath. Then he gently brushed her cheek before leaning down and kissing her. She returned the kiss, which lingered for quite a while.

"Very romantic. If it's alright with you, I'd love to restore it. That way, I'll have an excuse to keep visiting," he said with a playful glint in his eye. After that day, they became a couple, and it wasn't long before Knut moved in and became part of the family.

She told Knut about the unexpected pregnancy early one morning while they were lying in bed. "It looks like we'll have a new family member this winter," she said, turning toward him.

"Oh, have you finally decided on which dog you

want?" he asked, looking at her.

"No, that's not exactly what I meant," Maja smiled, stroking her belly, which already had a noticeable bump. "This is a different kind of family member, more the kind that's often called a spoiled last-born."

He finally understood what she meant. His eyes lit up, and he beamed at her. "Is it really true? We're going to be parents? Oh, how wonderful, my parents are going to be thrilled," he said, taking her in his arms. "I think the girls will be too."

After Maja and the boys bring out the furniture, she and Kjersti set the table. Not long after, the car with Knut and his parents drives into the yard. The elderly couple had embraced Maja and the girls from day one. Never a harsh word about anything, just joy that their son had found a life partner. And of course, they could see how happy he was. Together with his father, Knut goes to the barn and fetches the bench. Carefully, they carry it between them and place it in its rightful spot. They had covered it with a large sheet. The whole time Knut has been working on the bench, no one has been allowed to see it. Now, a proud Knut gets help from Laura with the unveiling.

"Dear everyone," he says solemnly, "Ever since I heard the romantic story behind this bench, I knew that restoring it was a task that required patience and love. After countless hours of work, it is with great pleasure that I hereby announce the love bench officially open."

Laura gently lifts off the sheet, revealing the bench in

all its glory. All the rotten boards and planks have been replaced, the old paint has been scraped off, and a new, fresh coat of dark green paint has been applied. The wrought iron has been polished and received a new layer of black paint. The inscription on the plaque is legible again, but it is the small, unopened velvet box that appears under the sheet that attracts the most attention.

"Come here, Maja," Knut says in a reverent tone. "Sit on the bench."

She does as she is told, but when Knut kneels in front of her, a small gasp escapes her, and she looks at him with wide eyes.

"My dear sweet Maja, you've stolen my heart. A stronger and braver person than you would be hard to find. Now I hope you'll let me take care of you and the little one that I'm so excited to meet. I love you. Will you marry me?" he asks, opening the box to reveal a beautiful gold ring with three small diamonds. Speechless with surprise, Maja stares at the ring. Then she looks at Knut.

"Yes," is all she can whisper. Then the cheers erupt. Knut's proposal and the news of the baby lead to tears of joy and many hugs. Maja, who in her wildest dreams had never imagined she could ever feel whole again, is happy.

The end

Author's Note

It's hard to believe that nearly ten years have passed since I first started working on this book. Back then, it didn't feel like the beginning of a novel—just a restless night when I couldn't sleep, scribbling down a few thoughts in a notebook. I had no idea those pages would lead to this.

A year earlier, I had a conversation with someone who shared a story that surprised me: he had been in an abusive relationship, but it was his ex-girlfriend who had been the violent one. It was rare for me to hear about female abuse in that context, but it opened my eyes to the reality that it happens.

Than one night, I wrote the first pages of this book, intending for Maja, my main character, to be the abusive one.

Time passed, and I got a job managing the Stordalen Hotel, a beautiful mountain hotel near the Stølsheimen area. It was during these years that I became captivated by the history of the Bjørn West resistance group, whose bravery is commemorated annually with a long, challenging hike. It's a major event in the region, and the more I learned about the story, the more it gripped me.

Bjørn West was a guerrilla unit that operated in the mountains of Stølsheimen during the last year of World War II. The group was established in 1944, when

Norwegian resistance fighters—many of them young men—were sent to this remote region to prepare for what seemed like the inevitable German surrender. However, the terrain of Stølsheimen, with its steep, rugged mountains, became a battleground as the Germans realized the threat posed by these guerrilla forces.

For months, Bjørn West fighters lived in harsh conditions, hiding in the mountains, launching surprise attacks, and using the area's natural defenses to evade capture. They were supplied by drops from Allied forces but lived under the constant threat of discovery.

In April 1945, just weeks before the war ended, the German forces launched a major offensive against the Bjørn West group. The resistance fighters, though heavily outnumbered, managed to hold their ground, fighting fierce battles in the mountains. The terrain worked to their advantage, but the losses were heavy. It's an amazing story of survival, resilience, and courage—one that left a deep mark on the region and its people.

During my time at the hotel, I had the privilege of interviewing one of the veterans from the Bjørn West group. He was reluctant to talk about his experiences during the war—it was clear that the memories still haunted him, even decades later. The scars, both physical and emotional, were still there. That interview stayed with me and deepened my desire to weave some of this incredible history into Maja's story.

I believe that as authors, we inevitably draw from our

own lives and personal histories when we write. I certainly have. My connection to the Masfjorden area runs deep—my mother spent many summers there as a child, and she used to tell me stories of the dances held in the old fish cabin and other local memories. I've also spent countless hours hiking in those mountains, following trails that the Bjørn West fighters once used. In fact, I once attempted a hike similar to the one Maja takes in the book, heading toward Voss. I ended up coming down in a different area, hitchhiking into town, but the landscape and the journey are etched into my memory.

There's also an old legend in the region about a hidden shelter in Stølsheimen, though not as elaborate as the one I created in the book. The real one was smaller, more of a hideaway beneath large rocks. But I've always been fascinated by the idea of hidden shelters, like the ones featured in survivalist programs where people prepare for all sorts of disasters. That idea played a role in shaping the fictional shelter in my story.

All the places I describe in the book are real. So is the story of Bjørn West. You can learn more about the guerrilla group by visiting the Bjørn West Museum in Matre or going to their webpage:

www.bjornwest.museumvest.no/en.

Everything else—the characters, the psychological drama—is purely fictional. As the story evolved, I decided I didn't want Maja to be the violent one. Instead, her story grew into something different, something that felt more authentic to the journey I wanted to explore.

Writing this story has been deeply personal for me. I know the land, the history, but most importantly, I have a deep empathy for the pain and suffering that can occur in relationships—whether it's the man or the woman who is the abuser.

This book is my way of telling a story that's both rooted in history and in the complexities of human relationships, and I hope it resonates with those who read it.

Lise Kristine Viken, Masfjordnes 2024

Thank you

A huge thank you to my parents, Sissel and Stein Viken, for inspiring the content of this book and for multiple rounds of proofreading of the Norwegian edition of this book. I deeply appreciate you both.

A heartfelt thank you to my wonderful daughter, Lisbeth Viken, for your invaluable consultation and corrections on the initial manuscript. Your ideas and insights are priceless.

A special thanks to Mari Nordås Lommelun for the fantastic manuscript consultation and for the Norwegian language editing. Without your sharp observations and thoughtful feedback, this book would not have become what it is today.

I am also deeply grateful to my incredible test readers (the Norwegian edition)—Sissel Heggertveit, Mari Karin Lesund, Anne-Lise Nordpoll, Tove Kayser (daughter of Bjørn West soldier Fredrik Kayser), and Gunn Berit Wiik—for your thorough, thoughtful reading and constructive feedback. You are all amazing!

Thank you so much to Rebecca Allen, whom I connected with on Reedsy, for your professional and precise proofreading and editing of the English version of this book. You did an excellent job!